A Mountain Leads Home

Most romance fans will find this book satisfying. It's best enjoyed next to a fireplace on a snowy day, preferably with some hot chocolate.

— S. PALMER, GOODREADS REVIEWER

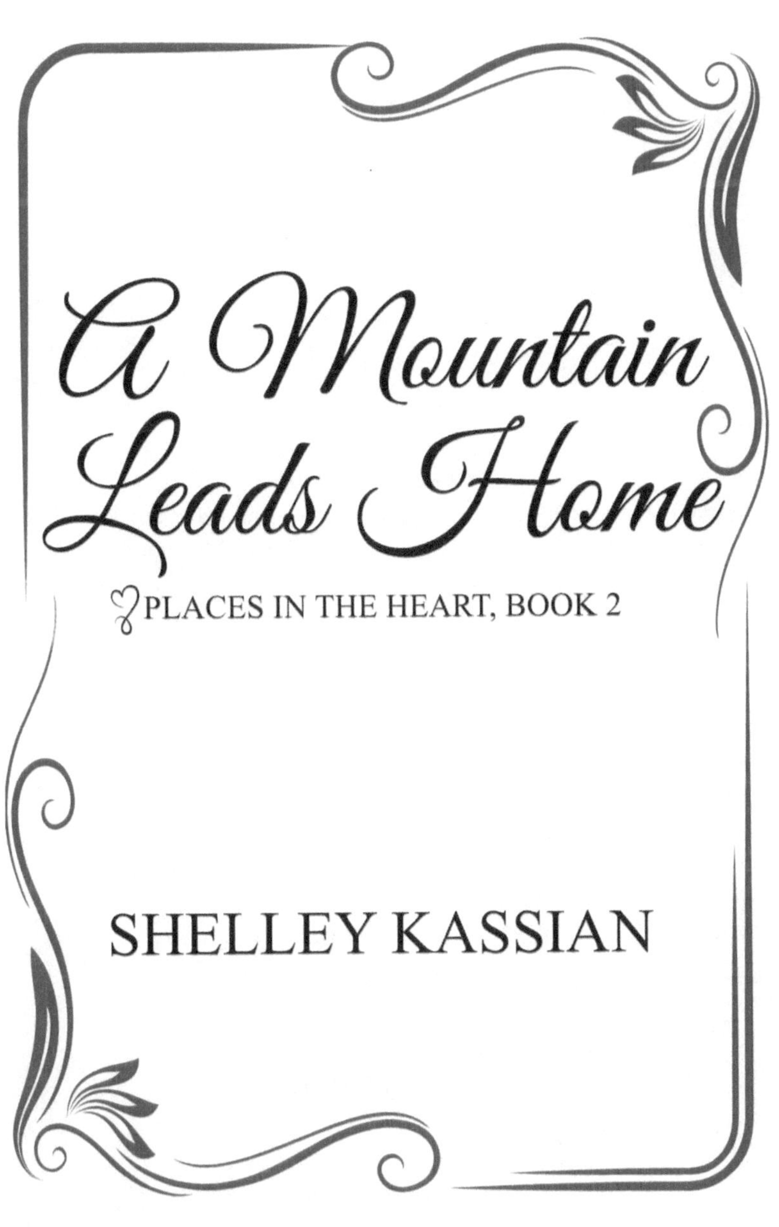

A Mountain Leads Home

PLACES IN THE HEART, BOOK 2

SHELLEY KASSIAN

DEDICATION

To my daughter and son-in-law:

William and Carrie Jewitt.

Thank you for the honor of sharing your love story.
I know you're nervous about the retelling,
but readers will understand that the story revealed within these
fictional pages arose from your mother's imagination.

ACKNOWLEDGMENTS

The premise of *A Mountain Leads Home* loosely narrates how an accident at a ski and snowboarding resort in Canada allowed my daughter and son-in-law to meet. I wish to acknowledge and thank William and Carrie for permitting me to fictionalize their journey as a couple as well as reviewing the first chapters prior to publication.

2022 has been a difficult year. Much thanks to author Katie O'Connor for her friendship, her support, and critique of this book. She asked me not to change a word, but then my editor found a few edits. Thank you, Ted.

I also want to recognize William's family in Australia who have become dear friends: George and Leone Jewitt, and their children/partners, Edward & Ally, and Jo & Rachel.

I adore the cover that 100 Covers created. The orange flowers add the right splash of wow. Orange is Carrie's favorite color.

And as always, my family: my husband Wayne, my son Shawn, Alicia & Trevor, and my mom Inez, for supporting my writing career.

CHAPTER ONE

THE SECOND WEEK OF NOVEMBER.

A rider on the Strawberry Express, Taylor Quinn mentally prepared himself to glide across winter white slopes. He aspired to ride, to snowboard, yet as his board dangled in the air, his left foot securely bound in the bindings, he wondered: *do I have the ability, the experience, or the skill to sail across these pristine runs?*

Soon, his angst-ridden thoughts wouldn't matter.

The chairlift climbed higher, transporting him toward the ride he'd been planning for months. The drive skyward only assisted his resolve while eyeing the expansive view. A painting could not adequately portray the Rocky Mountains frosted with white, or the skyline above the masterpiece, puffs of powder in a chalk-gray sky. *Amazing!* Taylor grinned like a child preparing to slide down a hill rather than a man fixing to ride a novice run.

I should be terrified. The slope seemed superior to Australian terrain, extraordinarily so, higher than what he'd imagined. Unlike any mountain range he'd ever seen before.

Mom would appreciate this view. Elizabeth…he remembered her cautionary words: *Please be careful, Taylor.* He laughed off the advice now as he had then at the Sydney airport. It didn't matter that her son had reached the age of thirty-five, motherly concern *always* traveled with him regardless of the destination.

He forced the memory to the corners of his mind while watching riders crisscrossing the slopes, some skiing, some snowboarding, right beneath the chairlift.

Someone jumped—

That's rad! That's amazing! Mom—sporting activities come with danger. Injury had found him before and no doubt would again, but what was life without risk, without living?

Ah…the gum tree…years ago. The view from its pea green branches were amazing until the stumble. The ground had been hard, too.

Taylor squeezed his fingers into a fist, dismissing broken bones as brisk winds shook the chairlift, causing knots to form in his gut. The height above this snow-covered ground made him queasier still, yet the frost in the air gave rise to wanderlust, an impulsive desire to conquer his inhibitions while listening to the wind whirr and the clickety clack of the sheave wheel as it rolled along the cable. The brittle cold nipped at his skin, his breath froze in the air, but now that he was here, bundled in winter gear, he couldn't wait to experience what he'd come here to do: Snowboard.

When he reached the top, he slid off the chairlift, his left boot bound in the bindings, his right foot free to propel himself and the board across the snow. He slid safely out of the path of other riders and waited for Luke to join him.

Riders left the lift and headed straight for the run. Not Taylor. He removed his goggles as sunshine poked through the clouds, the sunlight lit the slope. *Mom…if only you could see this beauty, this unexpected powder blue sky.* What a perfect picture. Taylor removed his phone from a zippered pocket in his down-filled jacket and took a few photos.

He put the phone away as a snowboarder swept past, making him question, *which path should I take*? Climb higher? Go left. Right?

Taylor slid farther to the right. He stretched his arms wide, his gloved fingers reaching toward the sky. Although the frost in the air nipped at his cheeks and filled his nostrils, he breathed deeply, tasting vitality and mountains fragrant with pine. It was true what other travelers said about Sunshine Ski Village. Pristine slopes and cold beauty existed in sharp contrast with each other, but harsh weather could not stop him from appreciating this winter wonderland.

Luke slid in beside him, his board caught an edge. He almost fell. "What are you waiting for, Taylor, praying for courage? Look at us." He pointed at himself. "I can't believe we're starting on a beginner run."

The comment amused Taylor as Luke was inclined to tease. Taylor removed his gloves and bent down, then placed his free boot in the binding. "Luke, you don't understand me. There's no harm in looking at the scenery. I'm ready for adventure, but life need not be rushed." He cranked the strap tightly, hoping he'd chosen a decent boot. "Snowboarding isn't the only factor thrilling me."

"Oh yeah, what else? The snow bunnies?" Luke asked, placing his free boot in the bindings, too. He rose upward and gently punched Taylor's arm. "We're here to have fun. Yes? If you're suggesting you're *not* in it for the adventure, you're lying."

Taylor grinned while putting his gloves on. "We're nothing like each other. I like to have fun as much as the next person, but unlike you, I'm not into showing off. I'm not an amateur either. I've snowboarded before. If I can balance on a surfboard, I can…"

"So, you've stood on a surfboard," Luke interjected, gesturing toward the slope. "Do these mountains look like the ocean? There's no surfing here. The ground's frozen. And…by the way, we're not flying down the runs at Thredbo either." Luke cleared his throat in an arrogant way. "These runs are next level. You haven't snowboarded in years."

Taylor shrugged. "Don't give me that tone. Mate, you sound like my mother."

"That's not fair."

"Look, it's rude to throw 'beginner' in my face," Taylor said, sighing. "You're bummed because you're ready for more challenging runs. No one's stopping you."

"Ah Taylor, I meant no offense. When we're more familiar with the slopes, tomorrow or the next day, let's try the runs on Goat's Eye Mountain. I've heard we'll experience the best runs on that slope."

"If you say so. What a strange name." Taylor shrugged, changing the subject while wondering why he'd traveled to

Canada with Luke. They'd known each other since grade school and their relationship had always been one-sided.

Luke pushed forward, sliding a bit. "Yeah, well, I'm not coming all this way without testing my abilities. I'm taking this ride if only to prove I still can."

Taylor nodded, envisioning flying across the slopes, too.

"It's good your mother's not here," Luke said, smirking, giving him the eye. "She'd remind you…"

"…of what, that I'm prone to accidents? It doesn't matter," Taylor said, laughing, swiping his hand back and forth as if to erase the comment. "If we waste time thinking about what *could* happen, we won't get in a few more runs."

"We should have been on the mountain earlier; too much partying last night. I work later," Luke said, sliding forward. "If you're finished staring at the trees and taking photos, can we ride already?"

"Sure. See you at the bottom." Taylor rose upward and stabilized his stance, equalizing his balance on the board. He placed the goggles over his eyes.

Like hell he'd see Luke at the base. His friend lived to chase thrills. Like a newly hatched turtle running across the sand on its trek toward the ocean, fear did not hinder Luke. He wouldn't wait, and Taylor didn't want to rush, deciding to take his time and ride at a leisurely pace, though he had to work tonight as well.

He nudged the board with his heel edge and moved cautiously while adjusting to the motion. He bent backward, squaring his shoulders and squatting slightly. He pushed his heel edge forward and came to a stop, mostly to ensure he could.

"Don't fall!" Luke called sarcastically, sliding past.

"Mate, try and keep up with me," Taylor replied, laughing, not taking his friend's warning or ill humor seriously, then he pushed off and began the run, trailing slightly behind Luke. The board moved smoothly beneath him, gliding across the snow. The force drove him onward like an airborne magic carpet hovering in the air.

Man, this sweeping motion filled Taylor with awe. In this moment, his desires personified the natural manner of a leisure activity as excitement surged through his veins, his heartbeat in his throat, riding the board across the snow amid the slopes of winter. Numerous thoughts pounded through his mind, biting cold, snow-spray against his cheeks, but none so great as this dash to pursue his sense of self.

He initiated a turn, cutting to the right, then arching to the left and sliding in the same direction. He dodged back and forth—*swish swish*, swooshing from side to side—snowboarding from the left to the right. He managed graceful 'S' turns, snaking through the snow. Not halfway through the run he slid onto his toe edge and stopped near a cluster of evergreens.

This mountain, this snowy amazing place. This is the best day of my life!

Someone yelled from behind: "Watch out!" Taylor muttered an apology as the rider rode past.

Maybe it wasn't wise to admire the mountain while on the run. He could appreciate the view from a safer vantage point, maybe later, while having lunch and a cold one at the chalet. He shifted the snowboard into motion again and followed behind the rider who had cursed him, seeing Luke ahead. *Who's praying now?* He'd stopped as well.

Taylor swooped right, then left, spraying snow into the air, his snowboard smearing through the snowfall like a knife spreading peanut butter. He managed his speed and dodged a boulder protruding from the snow. Excitement flowed through his veins.

It's okay to take risks. I don't want to play it safe. I want to run. I want to ride faster!

He picked up speed, neglecting to turn, racing down the slope. Though the run seemed a bit icy, more crystals than snow, nerve pushed him to the edge. Brazen courage rang in his ears, hearkening vitality and flashes of the younger self he'd been missing, encouraging him to ride faster.

He zigged. Zagged—and when Luke zoomed toward an opening in the evergreens, Taylor pursued, hurtling through the narrow gap.

What the heck? Taylor dug deeper. Life's short, too short not to take chances. When his board lifted off the snow and he flew— *"right on!"* —his daring overcame the thrust into the air like a bird leaping into flight. An epic joyride…until he struck the ground. Hard. He wobbled on the slope, losing his edge, but somehow managed to remain upright.

"Man, what a sic move!" Taylor shouted to Luke, thinking he probably hadn't heard him.

But now while maneuvering on a pathway between the trees, his equilibrium seemed compromised. The left boot had some slack. *Had the strap come loose?*

Should he stop?

Can I stop?

Taylor rode the snowboard at breakneck speed, trying not to concern himself with the board or his boot, but images of what could be flashed through his mind. Was he traveling too fast? His heartrate escalated while racing through a narrow snow-lined pathway, a tunnel where evergreens pressed in on all sides. He couldn't suppress the rising angst, the fear flowing through his veins, delivering weakness to his limbs. He struggled to breathe, wanting nothing more than to finish this run.

What if he collided with one of these trees, slipped in a tree well, or worse, smashed into a boulder? *I'll break my arm.* Taylor wobbled, finding insufficient space to maneuver.

Nah… He'd worry about the foot gear when he reached the bottom. It couldn't be much farther. He followed Luke as he'd done before, racing through the trees and down the slope. Luke leaped to the left. Seconds later, Taylor jumped to the right, grinning, spraying a wall of snow.

I've got this. But could he handle this board, these slopes? He was no more than a young soul stuck inside a thirty-five-year-old's body, seeking adventure, seeking thrills.

He leaned in the direction he wanted to ride, arching his heel edge too high, cutting too sharply. He whipped around a frozen tree trunk and fell forward, planting his face in the snow.

Whoosh!

His breath burst from his lungs.

The ground throttled his adventure, too rigid, too hard, the reverberation rang in his ears. He couldn't see, could not breathe. *What happened?* What hurt more, his face, his abdomen, or his pride? Taylor rolled onto his back, *gasping*, staring at the powder blue sky.

Luke trudged through the snow, marching toward him, carrying his snowboard. "What happened? I saw you lying on the ground."

"Don't know," Taylor said, panting, fighting an ache in his side. "Isn't it obvious?"

"I wanted to make sure you were okay. Are you all right, Tay?"

Taylor tried to breathe, but each inhalation hurt. Maybe the air knocked from his chest stimulated this sudden pain. He fixated on the stinging sensation in his lower extremities while lying on the frozen ground. The ache penetrated his lower limbs and nipped at his cheeks, his lips. He removed his gloves, his goggles, and wiped the snow off his face.

"Seriously, Taylor, you're paler than the snow. Are you okay?"

The clouds swirled, moving swiftly above him. He listened to raspy breathing while watching the sky. The wind whistled. A searing pain radiated in his abdomen, his left side. Had he hurt himself?

Luke knelt beside him, his hand on his shoulder. Where had he come from? "Taylor, talk to me." He sounded anxious. "Where does it hurt?"

"Did I fall?"

"Mate, you're lying on frozen ground. You were supposed to take it easy. The jump was sic, but you hit the ground like a rock."

"Incredible, flying through the air like that..." Taylor

groaned, grasping his side, smiling slightly. "The pain will pass. Help me stand."

"Seriously man, you sure? You don't look well."

"Yeah, I fell, but time's wasting. We work tonight. There's still time to ride. Though I'm ready for a meal, a cold one." He reached for Luke's outstretched hand. "Give me a moment to catch my breath."

"Okay, but only if you're sure." Luke grasped his hand.

Taylor nodded, but when he tried to rise to his feet, groaning, he collapsed on the frozen ground, doubling over in pain. He winced, his entire body sweating heat. "I need a minute for the pain to end."

Another snowboarder stopped. "Are you hurt? Do you need help?"

"I'm okay." But was he? The flat expression on Luke's face worried Taylor. He'd never seen his friend so serious.

Luke released his hand and knelt beside him in the snow. "My friend fell. He might be hurt. As a precautionary measure, the ski patrol should be notified."

"I have a cell phone. I'll make the call."

"No, seriously, guys, I'm fine," Taylor said, wincing. But he wasn't sure of anything. Although the bitter cold stifled his breath, heat blossomed on his face. When he tried to rise a second time, the pain stabbed him like a knife wedged in his gut. "Jeez! I can't believe this." Taylor grasped his side. "Why is this happening, today of all days?" he said with a grimace, expressing anger and frustration.

"It's probably nothing," Luke said, his tone shaky, "but it's best to get it checked out."

Taylor wondered if Luke sported a brave face for his sake because his eyes were dark with worry.

Once the snowboarder made the call, Taylor lay on the snow, looking around in confusion, in shock, ignoring the skiers and snowboarders who gawked at him as they slid past. When the ski patrol arrived, two members placed a neck brace around his neck and carefully maneuvered him onto a backboard on the toboggan. At least that's what they called the rescue sled that would carry him down the mountain.

"It's not far to the base," one ski patrol member said. "Don't worry. We'll take good care of you. We'll assess your medical needs and have you back on the hill in no time."

Taylor hoped their words were true, but their pinched expressions had him uneasy. They'd seen many injuries. Maybe they assessed the situation without knowing the extent of his injury, but once they had him on an examination table at the resort's emergency room, their assertions only became clearer. The poking and prodding yielded suspicious results. When someone laid a hand on his abdomen near his ribs, Taylor groaned, nearly screaming for the pain. It was decided he should be examined at the hospital in Banff. As an ambulance pulled away from the resort with him inside, Taylor knew he'd suffered a significant injury. His head buzzed, his limbs ached, and suddenly dizzy, he worried he might vomit or faint.

His mother's plea played in his mind like a broken record: *Please be careful...*

Why hadn't he listened? Why hadn't he avoided the jump, the gap in the trees? This was only his first day on the mountain, the first run of the season and potentially…his last.

Damn it!

Taylor swore silently while sharing a new ride with paramedics. The ambulance left the resort with him inside, sad and despondent, lying inside its steel sheath. He tried to ignore the soreness in his gut, his focus shifting to loss. Was his snowboarding adventure over? What should he do now? Taylor closed his eyes, placing his hand on his forehead, not ready to accept this fate.

CHAPTER TWO

TWO DAYS LATER.

Ugh. This job has me acting like a robot. In the middle of a hospital hallway, Sarah grasped her aching head and raked her fingers through her hair. Suffering exhaustion and coping with burnout, how could she help patients when she couldn't help herself?

A caring and consummate professional, Sarah Evans knew she must adapt to an ever-changing workload, coping with patient needs, job struggles and time constraints. More than anything, a too heavy workload had her yearning for freedom.

How would she find this missing ingredient?

A partner—Love.

The short-staffed unit experienced anxious and slapdash days. *Ding. Ding. Ding*—Patient call bells rang continuously.

Sarah sighed, standing beside another patient's room, the only patient who hadn't pressed their call bell this morning.

Why? Taylor Quinn had suffered a grade two ruptured spleen. Surely a patient recovering from an embolization procedure needed assistance. *Pain meds?* Outside room ten, Sarah searched within herself for the mental fortitude to do her job.

I don't have a choice. Breathing a sigh, Sarah entered.

She didn't comprehend what she'd expected to find, but this man, the patient nurses were gossiping about...well, he smiled at her. Sarah sucked in a breath, staring at him as if she'd never seen a patient before, let alone a man. Slim and trim with an athletic build. Wavy, dark blond hair and metallic blue eyes: the color of a cloudless sky or a deep blue sea. She swallowed her nerve as the silence stretched...a moment too long, but the light burning in his eyes, a sight she would describe as wondrous, maybe kind.

She shook off his magnetic appeal and stepped toward him, pausing at the foot of his bed. "Hi, I'm Sarah, your day nurse." She pivoted, walked to the whiteboard and grabbed a marker, printed her name on the surface and then faced him again. "I'm here to take your vital signs."

Taylor stared at her in a curious, thoughtful manner. "Hi, Sarah. It's lonely without visitors. Thanks for stopping by."

Her brows rose. *Thank you? It's my job to care for you.* "You're welcome, but I've only printed my name on the board. Compliments should wait until I've given more than casual conversation." She grinned.

"You're here. I'm...grateful."

Sarah approached the foot of his bed, reached for the medical clipboard and briefly scanned the patient's information, all the while thinking about the gossip. *Taylor*

Quinn. They're right, he is handsome. Though he looks like a sailor tossed up from the sea. The name suits him.

"You're from Australia?"

"Yeah, Sydney. I'll probably be heading home soon." He glanced at his abdomen, frowning. "I was excited to experience my mountain holiday, but I fell on the first day, on the first run. Can you believe it? What dumb luck. My plans ended abruptly." She ached for him. His voice held so much melancholy.

"I'm sorry," Sarah said, trying to sound positive. "No one expects an accident. Your disappointment is understandable. You're here on vacation?"

What was wrong with her? She not only felt like a robot, but sounded like one, too. She needed to take his vital signs and then proceed to the next patient, certainly not entertain mindless chatter, but she remained where she stood, holding the clipboard tightly, gaping at this man, this Australian with interesting eyes, compelling eyes that stared at her, encouraging her to offer more time than she had to give. He looked through her as if he held some kind of superpower. What a ridiculous thought given he'd suffered a ruptured spleen. Marvel characters didn't rupture anything.

"The vacation ended with me lying flat on my back." The first sign of injury, *pain*, pulled across his face. He winced, his brow creasing. "The holiday of a lifetime. I planned for it over several months."

Sarah pulled a pen from her pocket and tapped it against the clipboard, regaining her composure. "I'm sure it was great until the moment of impact." She eyed the paperwork and then the patient. "It says here you took a fall while snowboarding."

He winced. Maybe the trauma had given him a flashback. "The run challenged my snowboarding skills. One minute I was having the time of my life, and the next, I was face-planting in the snow."

"You're lucky your nose didn't break."

"Never thought of that," Taylor said, shaking his head. "Once I'm healed, I'm not sure whether I should snowboard again, at least not in Canada."

"It's a dangerous winter sport and our mountains have high elevations. Unfortunately, I see many snowboarding injuries." Sarah's lips curved into a half-smile. "You'll recover. You'll ride again. You don't look like the type who would quit."

"You're right. I don't frighten or give up easily." Taylor smirked. "This isn't a simple injury, but I'd like to snowboard again."

Sarah edged closer. "After an accident, my mother always advised to walk it off, get up and do it again," Sarah said. She raised her hand and issued a firm warning. "However, I'm not suggesting you should snowboard next week. Contact sports are not recommended for the next few months, as I'm sure the surgeon told you. But once you're fully recovered, get on the board and ride again, otherwise you'll lose your confidence."

"Do you know what you're talking about? Have you experienced serious injuries?"

"Me?" Sarah shrugged. "Minor ailments. A twisted ankle, a burned hand. I don't take risks. Working here," she said, giving him a firm stare, "the trauma unit motivates caution rather than needless risk."

Stop talking. Focus on the reason you're here—your job. "How are you feeling? Are you experiencing pain?"

Taylor moved his hand to his abdomen. Sarah watched slim fingers stroking the blue hospital gown. "My left side is tender," Taylor said with a grimace.

"That's normal. It's only been two days since your procedure. Rate your pain level on a scale of zero to ten, zero meaning you're in no pain, ten meaning you're in a lot of discomfort."

"Probably a three or a four. I'm slightly uncomfortable."

Sarah studied Taylor's dry eyes, his pale face. She knew the warning signs. If pain unsettled Taylor, he suppressed the discomfort. It seemed like he might faint, yet he didn't complain. Why were some patients strong and others weak, whining and complaining, never giving her a moment of peace? Sarah didn't want a weak man in her life and knew she shouldn't look at Taylor in his dour blue hospital gown as if he were a potential candidate. The man lying on the hospital bed presented as *her* patient, and though she cared for him—as a nurse who attends to practical treatments—they shared some sort of connection: strict attentiveness and natural human emotion.

What's wrong with me?

A hospital room wasn't the place to consider relationships, and certainly not with a patient. Interactions of an intimate nature challenged ethical and moral boundaries.

If only I had my freedom. If only I had time to find someone, someone worthy of my love.

Sarah sighed, then wrote the number five on the paperwork. She'd be single for the rest of her life.

"Is it time for my medication?" Taylor asked. "I don't remember when I had it last."

Sarah glanced at her watch. "It's time. You probably should have had it half an hour ago." Sarah placed the medical clipboard in the holder. "Give me a minute. I'll get your medication and return shortly."

Sarah left Taylor's room and proceeded to a secure area where she retrieved Tylenol with Codeine #3 from a medicine cabinet. Then she returned to Taylor's room and gave him his medication.

"I'LL TAKE YOUR TEMPERATURE," Sarah said.

The nurse placed the thermometer on his forehead and swept the instrument toward his left ear. Taylor didn't concern himself with the medical task as the nurse intrigued him more. With her standing this close, he couldn't dismiss her beauty. A pretty face, brown eyes flecked with gold, and mussed brown hair highlighted with light-colored hues and pulled into a ponytail. Peach scrubs complemented her rosy complexion. What healthy male wouldn't be attracted to her? Heaven help him, he didn't want to appear rude or overbearing, studying a woman in an inappropriate way, so he fixed his attention on her slender fingers.

"Your temperature's normal. Let's check your oxygen rate." She placed a pulse oximeter on his index finger.

Taylor noticed lines and dark circles beneath her eyes. "You're tired."

"What?" A surprised look shadowed her eyes.

"The lines beneath your eyes. The paleness of your skin."

"It's winter, everyone's pale." She shrugged. "I'm trying to make a beauty statement without the benefit of makeup. I mean, who has time for makeup in this place?" She removed the oximeter from his finger. "But seriously, fatigue challenges the staff on Unit 44. No one cares about me or other nurses' delivering healthcare on this unit. In this place, patient needs come first, as it should be."

I care about you, Taylor mused.

The workload seemed unbalanced, unfair. Taylor wanted to tell Nurse Sarah she mattered; her health needs were as essential as patient care. How could she attend to the injured if her well-being was compromised? But he had no knowledge of the nurse or the situation. He felt uninformed and naïve while saying, "Maybe you should take some time off." As if days off or holidays would solve the problem. Not likely.

"I could use a vacation." She looked at him in a meaningful way. Her dreamy look hit him hard. He wanted to learn more about her. He wanted to give her an ingredient missing from her life: contentment.

"Where would you go?" Taylor asked.

Sarah smiled, her fatigue transforming into a dreamy expression. He liked this happier look.

"A hot place with a beach, a book and a lounge chair. A mojito in my hand, the sun on my face and the ocean in the distance." She seemed contemplative and breathed as if smelling salty air. She glanced away, playing with her ponytail, and looked at the hospital window as if yearning to escape this place, clearly thinking about summer weather, but then she returned her focus to him. "I bet the beaches in Australia are nice."

"I suppose they're appealing for the average traveler. Honestly, I haven't considered whether the beaches in Sydney are holiday worthy or not, and I've spent a fair bit of time near the ocean, either jogging on wet sand or waiting to catch a wave. How's my oxygen rate?"

"Oh wow, I'm sorry. I got caught up in the idea of vacationing," Sarah said, blushing. "Ninety-five. You're breathing."

She grasped his wrist. Her strength, three tiny fingers probing for a pulse, stimulated his masculinity as much as his heart. It raced. He tried to understand: a nurse's role; her kindness, tenderness, caused his face to flush. He looked at the woman, a pretty woman who stood so near to him he smelled the tang of oranges. Or was it vanilla perfume?

After a while, she removed her hand and grasped the clipboard. "Ninety-five beats a minute," she said, notating the number.

"Is that high?" Taylor took a breath, swallowing.

She peered at him, then kept on writing. "A bit. We expect higher pulse rates after some procedures."

"But my *'obliteration'* took place two days ago."

Sarah smirked, eyeing him in a humorous way. When the corners of her lips rose upward, Taylor knew he'd articulated the word incorrectly. "Your em-bol-i-za-tion procedure?" she said, giggling.

Embarrassed, Taylor hung his head, not knowing how to respond.

Sarah touched his wrist. "Oh dear, it's okay. It's a big word." Dear? Did she mean him? Her voice was saccharine, sugary sweetness, and edged with laughter she couldn't suppress. Had she really called him *dear*? Taylor was ashamed to admit he liked the acknowledgement and appreciated the humor. It distracted him from his painful situation.

Taylor placed his forehand against his forehead. "Oh. My. God. I'm so embarrassed. I can't believe I messed that up."

Sarah shook her head, smothering her laughter. "Taylor, I need to visit other patients. I'll come by later to ensure your pain meds are administered on time. Perhaps take you for a walk around the unit. It's time to get out of bed."

"I'd like to leave this bed." Not only to exercise but also to see the nurse, Sarah, again. He found himself wanting to leave the room and walk beside her, but he had patience. He could wait.

Sarah's brows rose as if she'd read his mind. "This isn't a date."

"It could be. I'm single, dear."

Though her face tensed and her lips slackened, she didn't speak.

Taylor immediately regretted the retort, sensing he'd misread the patient/nurse relationship. But the apparent blunder didn't stop him from giving serious thought to asking the nurse for a date, and her beauty wasn't the only inspiring factor. There was something about Sarah. A quality, compassion, that drew him to her. He wanted to pursue this mysterious connection.

She blushed. "I'm single, but you're my patient. Please, don't get any ideas."

It never occurred to Taylor that Sarah might have rules to comply with; all he saw was a pretty woman with a kind disposition, and with her face blooming, her words were not at all convincing.

"No one else will escort me around the unit. I don't have friends here."

"Oh yeah? The guy who came by yesterday, who was he?" *Came by yesterday?* How had she obtained that information?

"My friend, Luke. He traveled with me from Sydney, but he's working at Banff Sunshine Village, the ski and snowboard resort. He doesn't have a vehicle. It's difficult for him to get to the city," Taylor said, frowning. Luke didn't have time for him. When he wasn't snowboarding, he was working.

"It must be hard on your family. They're so far away."

Taylor sighed. "I have not informed my parents about the accident. I haven't had the courage to tell them about the fall let alone the injury. My mother…"

"…probably told you to tread carefully. Am I right?" Sarah grabbed the blood pressure cuff and placed it above his elbow on his left arm.

"She'll be disappointed."

"If she's like most mothers, she'll be worried and glad to hear your voice." Sarah turned on the blood pressure machine. "You should call her."

The band constricted his arm. The pressure hurt. "You're right. I'll text her this afternoon. I'd do it this morning but there's a time difference."

"I'm sure she'd appreciate a phone call. She'll realize you're okay when she hears your voice."

"You're a nurse. I can tell you're good at talking to people. You could call her. You could tell her." He hoped Sarah would take this responsibility away from him. He dreaded talking to his mother.

"Me? I don't think so," Sarah said, laughing, her voice the sound of music. "My responsibilities don't include *caving-in* to a patient's personal needs."

He reached for her hand and touched it slightly. "Oh yeah? Well, I'd be in your debt, forever grateful."

Sarah didn't protest his touch, didn't shrink away from the prospect; her eyes brightened, and her cheeks flamed pink. Yet she shook her head, pulling away. "Taylor…" she sounded frustrated, with herself, with him maybe, but he liked the way she said his name. "…contacting your mother is beyond my scope of responsibility."

"Sarah, I understand, but it would mean the world to me. I've had accidents before. My mom won't accept the truth if I make the call. If a nurse delivers the news, she'll realize I'm recovering. She respects professionals like you."

"Your friend didn't have the foresight to inform your family?"

"No," Taylor declared, shaking his head. "I made Luke promise not to tell my secret. I wouldn't permit it."

"That's terrible. Someone should notify your family." Sarah retrieved her phone. "What's your mother's number?"

"You mean, you'll do it?"

Her brows rose. She looked at him curiously. "Give me the number before I change my mind."

"Would you like mine as well?"

Sarah seemed surprised. She literally took a step away from his bed. Taylor didn't understand why he had asked such a daring question, but he gritted his teeth, waiting for a response, hoping she'd say *yes*. Sarah didn't respond for several seconds. Taylor held his breath, waiting—Maybe a man hadn't made a pass at her before, maybe his question had shocked her into silence.

"Taylor Quinn," Sarah said, taking a deep breath. They shared a connection, he could tell by the earnestness in her eyes, but Taylor worried his outspokenness had hurt their newfound relationship. Had he offended her? What had he done?

Sarah sighed. "I'm ready. Give me your mother's number."

Taylor shared the number and Sarah added it to her contact list. Giving up wasn't part of his nature. *There are other ways to make contact.*

"Okay, maybe it's too soon for us to exchange phone numbers. Are you on Facebook? What if we became Facebook friends?"

An LPN entered the room.

Sarah shook her head. "I'll come back later to take you for exercise."

When she stared at him as if he was behaving like a difficult patient giving her a hard time, maybe more emotional trauma than she could manage, she left the room so swiftly Taylor wondered whether she'd keep her promise. Though he knew she'd return, for one reason or the motive that mattered most: Sarah Evans was *his* nurse.

CHAPTER THREE

Inside the staffroom, Sarah worried about Taylor as much as her job. There were never enough hours in a day to complete her tasks. Another shift had ended without accomplishing her goals. With seriously ill patients requiring care, in an entire shift she'd only seen Taylor twice. The reasons were valid. The trauma unit was in crisis mode: an abdominal bleed, breathing difficulties, high fever, infection, pain…patient needs were piling up, one on top of the other like a heavy weight, but the workload hadn't stopped her from considering the patient in room ten.

Taylor Quinn—he'd lodged himself in her thoughts as if she were experiencing a compulsive habit. Like chocolate, a glass of wine, or a strong cup of coffee, Sarah couldn't stop thinking about him, which only added to her guilty conscience.

Had she neglected proper and acceptable beliefs? *I shouldn't think about him like this.*

There hadn't been time for the rehabilitative walk. She

hadn't called Taylor's mother either. Sarah sighed. Why had she made the promise in the first place? Personal requests were not part of her duties, so why were her thoughts preoccupied with guilt?

Sarah reached inside her locker and grabbed her purse, her backpack and lunch bag, then traipsed to the doorway, dog-tired, prepared to leave the staff room and the hospital. But when she reached the unit's exit, prepared to walk to the elevator, she knew she couldn't leave the hospital without keeping her promise.

Damn it.

She leaned against the wall, clenching her hand, her posture stiff, her shoulders aching, pain radiating through her and settling in the small of her back. The fatigue, heavier than the insignificant weight of the backpack held in her hands. She wanted to escape the trauma and go home, to sleep…but she couldn't do it.

A promise made pledged an oath to a promise kept.

Should she call Taylor's mom? Yes, of course, she'd be a failure if she didn't.

Sarah resigned herself to returning to the patient lounge. Once she arrived, she sat on a leather chair and ignored other health professionals or visitors as they walked past. She retrieved her cell phone from her purse and let the backpack slip from her hand to the floor.

Long-distance charges would be incurred on her next cell phone bill. Was it expensive placing a call to Australia? It didn't matter. The call was necessary, so she researched the required long-distance numbers and dialed, listening to the ring tone until someone answered.

"Hello?"

"Hi, this is Sarah Evans. I'm a nurse in Calgary, Canada. Am I speaking to Taylor Quinn's mother?"

"Yes…" Mrs. Quinn's voice lowered as the probable meaning for the call took hold.

"I'm calling to inform you, that Taylor…"

Sarah heard an audible gasp. "What happened?" Mrs. Quinn asked, her voice breaking. "What happened to my son?"

"Mrs. Quinn, Taylor's okay, but he had an accident at the ski resort."

"No—" she said, her voice strangled, racing toward panic. Sarah could well imagine a mother's concern while waiting for a response. Mrs. Quinn said, "I asked him to be careful. Are you certain he's okay? Why hasn't he called me?"

Sarah placed her hand against her forehead, searching for strength to guide this conversation, however, telling a mother, a father, or an entire family difficult news could unnerve the strongest individuals. She took a deep breath, realizing Taylor's mother dwelled in a country thousands of miles away. She couldn't support her son or visit her son to appreciate he was okay. Sarah didn't want her to worry.

"Taylor's in a bit of discomfort, but he's healing. He doesn't want you to worry, which is why he asked me to inform you."

"Knowing my son, there's always reason for concern. What happened?"

"I've only just met Taylor, but you know how much he enjoys snowboarding."

"He fell, didn't he."

"Yes," Sarah replied, her tone soft and controlled. "It wasn't a terrible fall. Your son didn't suffer broken bones, nor did he experience a concussion, though he did rupture his spleen."

"Oh no…this is similar to his older brother," Mrs. Quinn whispered, her voice forlorn, quiet and strongly accented. Sarah almost couldn't distinguish the words.

"His brother suffered the same injury?"

"Yes, in Colorado. It happened years ago."

"Then you understand the injury but let me explain the procedure. Taylor had a grade two ruptured spleen. Enough of an injury to give him some serious internal bleeding. But the surgeon performed an embolization procedure. It was successful. The bleeding has stopped. It's been two days…"

"You waited two days to tell me?"

Sarah heard the disappointment in Mrs. Quinn's voice. She knew the irritation arose from a son's injury and had nothing to do with her. "I only met your son today. I can't explain why Taylor hasn't notified you, but having been his nurse, I assure you, he's recovering. In fact, I'll see him shortly."

"Oh, I see."

"I'll make sure he calls."

"I'd appreciate that, Miss…"

"You may call me Sarah."

"Thank you, Sarah." The voice wobbled. It sounded like a mother might cry.

"Please, don't worry," Sarah said, swallowing, knowing she had to say goodbye. But before this call concluded she wanted to ease a mother's concern. "I must go. I'll make sure Taylor calls."

"Should his father and I come to Canada?" Mrs. Quinn exclaimed.

"Where, to Calgary?"

"Yes."

"You should discuss travel decisions with your son. But as I said, I'll ensure he calls. Have a good day, Mrs. Quinn. Try not to worry."

"Sarah?"

"Yes…"

"Please take care of Taylor. He's my youngest boy. He's special to me."

Sarah hadn't planned on making promises she couldn't keep but alleviating a mother's concern appealed to her sense of duty. "I'll do my best."

"Give him our family's well-wishes, tell him we love him."

"I'll do that."

Sarah entered Taylor's room carrying an orange popsicle. When he looked at her with a lopsided smile and a wicked grin, his contentment made the effort worthwhile, but his expression quickly shifted to one of disappointment. He shook his head.

"Where have you been?" Taylor asked, pointing at the white board. "Notice the name on the board. It no longer says Sarah. Hours have passed since you were here." He pouted like a child yet smirked as she came closer.

"Hey, I apologize for not coming sooner, but that's what happens at the end of a nurse's shift. The name changes, but hopefully the same level of care is offered." She was sorry. She wanted to make it up to him. "I brought you a peace offering."

His eyebrows rose. "An ice-block?"

"Is that how they label popsicles in Australia?"

Taylor nodded, then folded his arms across his chest. "It'll take more than one ice-block to make me happy."

"I didn't expect a poor attitude," Sarah said, managing a brief laugh. "I'm here now."

"I see that."

"I couldn't visit sooner, but that doesn't mean I didn't think of you."

"You thought of me?"

"Yes, of course. I think about *all* patients." Though at this moment he was the only patient she wanted to assist. The only one she sought to administer care. *Why?* Her shift ended an hour ago. "Did Arnel visit? He told me he would."

"We had a good talk. We shared friendly conversation. As it happens, we have similar interests. Arnel likes sports and snowboarding as much as me, but he's not you and his name's not Sarah."

How did Sarah respond to the sugary tone in which he said her name? Dripping with sweetness and in direct contrast to the contact sports. The conversation was as gummy as the melting popsicle. Orange color dripped between her fingers, sticky fingers. Tacky situations caused her head to ache. What should she do with this patient? Maybe she should have set off for home at the end of her shift. *No*, that's not what she wanted. She was grateful she'd chosen to stay.

"Do you want the ice-block? It's melting."

"Sure. Pass it over."

Sarah gave Taylor the sugary treat, then approached the sink to wash her hands. "Taylor, I'm sorry." She was sorry. "I can't change what happened. Over the course of the day, patients sicker than you needed my care, but I didn't want to leave the hospital without keeping my promise." She eyed him. Her decision apparently gave him joy as he smiled.

"I'm sorry, Sarah." Taylor licked the popsicle. "I appreciate your kindness."

"I'm on my own clock now, so we can walk for as long as you want." She glanced at him. "For as long as your strength holds out."

"Seriously, Sarah, I understand. I don't want to keep you. Go home. Rest. You were tired this morning and the shadows beneath your eyes have not lessened."

"I'm still tired," Sarah said, soaping her hands. "But a promise is a promise. We'll walk after you've finished your treat."

She heard him crunching the ice. Taylor consumed the ice-block in three bites. "You're fast."

"I'm ready."

It wasn't improper or brazen to escort Taylor around the unit, but Sarah knew spending time with a patient, after hours, might be an ethical violation. Yet, she disregarded her guilt-ridden thoughts and led him along the corridor. After all, who would question her decision? It wasn't the first time she'd stayed late to help a patient. But this moment held unique appeal.

Why would she shoulder this risk?

Confused, Sarah struggled with the emotional boundaries. She glanced at the stoic man walking beside her, her hand resting lightly on his elbow. Was she experiencing sentimental feelings because she cared about Taylor's health and well-being, and wanted to offer her nursing skills? After hours? Or had hidden wants and needs, motivated by his potent vigor and brawn physique, challenged her intellect? Though self-evident, the attraction warred with her fluttering heart, further encouraging awareness.

They passed the nursing station. The head nurse at the desk studied her in a curious manner. Sarah shrugged her shoulders in a dismissive way and kept on walking, moving past the higher authority and out of the unit.

At present, she didn't care what anyone thought.

"Where are you taking me?" Taylor asked, massaging his side, leaning forward slightly. Was he in pain?

She paused and grasped his shoulder. Taylor gazed at her hand, the place where she touched him, studying her inquisitively.

She shifted her hand to his elbow. "Are you hurting, Taylor? Maybe we should return to your room. Maybe we've walked far enough." Maybe her guilty conscience clouded logical thinking. She was least motivated to escort Taylor to his room.

"No way, I waited all day for this." He paused in the hallway. "I need to rest for a moment. I'll be fine."

"Sure. Why don't we sit in one of those chairs," Sarah said, leading Taylor to a leather couch near the unit's entrance, then assisting him to sit. Sarah sat in a chair beside Taylor.

"I'm concerned about my health. I'm still experiencing abdominal pain."

Taylor grasped his left side. His face scrunched; the color drained from his face. He seemed like a scared kid. The behavior wasn't abnormal, many adults were uncomfortable in the hospital.

"You're healing. You're coping with a serious injury, but it's only been two days. You need time to mend, time for your health and strength to return to normal."

"If you say so. I wish I hadn't been hurt in the first place. I wish I was breathing mountain air." He closed his eyes and Sarah wondered if he was visualizing the run and the joy he had experienced while sailing across the snow, or maybe the trauma came to mind.

For most patients, coping with trauma and subsequent pain, or accepting how they were hurt, caused constant worry. Pain reliever could not ease all of life's letdowns. Though Sarah understood where the regret arose from. In time, he'd focus on the future, not the past.

"I called your mom."

"You did?" He gave her a surprised look. "How did she take the news?"

"She expressed her concern, and her love for you," Sarah

said, her lips rising into a half-smile. "I tried to reassure her you were okay."

"Am I okay?" Taylor's facial expression hardened into a serious mien. "What if the bleeding begins again, what if I bleed out?"

Sarah leaned toward Taylor. She grasped his arm. "Mr. Quinn, this is your nurse's order: Focus on the positive. You're healing. The pain will lessen with each passing day."

He glanced at her hand. "I'm grateful for your nursing skills. You're a good person, Sarah. It's kind of you to help me, after hours. Good of you to call my mom."

Sarah gave Taylor her best commanding stare, then released her hold. "I gave your mom terrible news. The recent events probably left her feeling overwhelmed. No one wants to learn a family member's been hurt. You need to call your mom."

Taylor's face scrunched. "Well, thank you for the lecture," he said, wincing. "I'll do as you've advised as soon as my voice stops shaking. My mother would notice the slightest tremor. It's the real reason I asked for your help."

Sarah studied his eyes, blue eyes lined with worry. She nodded, wanting to comfort him. "This will pass. You'll recover, you'll snowboard again. Can you focus on the positive?"

"I can, when I'm with you."

"Taylor—" Sarah knew she had to say it, though she didn't want to say it: "I'm your nurse."

His brows rose in a surprised way, like she wasn't his nurse and he wasn't her patient. Two friends sitting beside each other sharing a friendly conversation. His facial expression shifted to one of concern. "I appreciate that. It's just…I'm in a foreign country. I'm alone in a hospital, in a trauma unit. My only friend works at the ski resort. My family is in Australia." He raised his hands. "I promised my mother I wouldn't get hurt. Look at me," he said, touching his side, "I'm a wreck, a babbling baby. And as if my situation isn't distressing enough…I'm alone."

At the mention of his mother, Sarah remembered her promise to take care of Taylor. She recognized something else, too. Family and friends were an important part of her life, and though she wasn't alone, not like Taylor, loneliness consumed her.

Sarah wanted more from life than nursing. She desired love. Was she unlovable? Was she worthy of someone's love? This wasn't the best time or place to consider such sentiments.

"Your mother loves you. She told me so. And you're not alone." Sarah grasped his hand and squeezed. "Your nurse is with you."

Taylor studied her like a beaten soldier, solemn and afraid. He wasn't a warrior. A man a few years younger than herself, but why should age matter? She couldn't dismiss the warmth in his eyes, his lost eyes, a look revealing either the fear of being alone or the discomfort of his wounded spleen. The thought he might be in pain shook her to reality.

"It must be time for your pain meds," Sarah said.

"I don't need pills."

"I don't want you to suffer."

"I want to leave this place, to finish what I began…on the mountain."

"Once you're stronger you could return to the mountain, even if it's to explore the area in a different way."

Taylor frowned. Her words hadn't made a difference, hadn't given him hope. "Would you come with me? Would you take me?"

"Taylor," Sarah said, her tone asserting a firm truth, "we've had this discussion about my role in your life." Sweet heavens, she was his nurse. Regardless of their emotional state, these feelings for each other were maturing too fast.

When Sarah released Taylor's hand, he grasped her hand and held it firmly. Sarah studied his handhold while perusing the wistfulness in his eyes, eager to help this patient in ways she'd never helped others, and despite her reservations, her assistance transformed into a deeper connection.

"Roles change all the time," Taylor said. "People meet in different ways. There's nothing wrong with how we met."

Sarah felt overcome with emotion. The tension squeezed at her heart. "We're strangers."

"Sarah, I've traveled places. I've met many people. If holidays have taught me anything about human behavior, it's this: everyone's a stranger until they first meet. Look, there's something happening here. A vibe, an attraction. Does that make sense to you?"

"Maybe," Sarah said quietly.

"You and I, we can be friends, or more than friends, if you're willing to see me as something more than a patient."

Taylor released his handhold, and Sarah, having been acutely aware of his touch, missed the warmth. She flexed her fingers, wishing he still held her hand. Taylor aroused an emotional response that blossomed on her face and caused sweeter thoughts to swirl in her mind and in her heart. *What just happened?*

"I understand what you're trying to say," Sarah said.

"Do you?"

Sarah inhaled deeply. "I have my profession to consider. Our conversation borders on awkward, Taylor."

She glanced away, reeling from controversial desires and a viewpoint she couldn't negate. It didn't matter that her intelligence, her sense of compassion, and pure human chemistry compelled her to challenge professional beliefs; the medical profession said a nurse shouldn't be attracted to a patient. Ethical rules must be respected. Sarah looked at Taylor, his handsome face, his easy-going manner, and she couldn't escape the connection, the attraction, and furthermore, didn't want to deny her emotions.

Why should she?

Taylor smiled. "Tell me about it."

Sarah shook her head, smiling as well. A flush blooming on her cheeks. "You're challenging my sense of right and wrong." She stroked Taylor's hand, mesmerized by his bright eyes. "Is there an attraction passing between us? Or am I losing my mind, sensing an emotion that doesn't exist?"

Taylor nodded. "A fondness affected me from the start. It's unexpected, but yes, there's chemistry. I hear you regarding the subject of rightness, but they don't teach romance in school. We can't measure affairs of the heart with a ruler."

He gave Sarah the sweetest smile, leading her to question: what had the admission, her truth, a confession of innermost desires, cost her? The price could challenge her job but also contribute to a more important interest, her romantic self.

CHAPTER FOUR

"Oh dear." Sarah shook her head in disbelief. What had she confessed? What trouble would she face for the admission?

One day later, she sat at her kitchen table, tapping her fingers against the glass tabletop. Taylor pressed into her thoughts. Why couldn't she get him out of her thoughts? Deep inside, she knew why. Like a fish drawn to a hook, a handsome Australian had influenced the part of herself desiring masculine company. No—her emotions were motivated by brawn and muscle, consistent with a woman who desired a partner.

But their relationship was developing too fast. Sarah didn't have a good track record with men and Taylor had only been her patient for one day.

One day.

Yet his spoken words, his eyes, and well-mannered nature consumed her thoughts. His release from hospital would come in days. If they were to remain in contact, a means to communicate was necessary.

Facebook? Instagram? What if Taylor sent her a friend request? How would she respond if such a message appeared on her screen? How would she respond?

The situation presented difficulty. Though Sarah had strong beliefs and held herself to high professional standards, violating ethical values could pose a risk. If she put job standards aside and thought logically, considering humane reasons to befriend Taylor, her emotional and physical well-being came to mind.

She wondered what he looked like without clothes on. She shook her head, putting her hand to her forehead. *What is wrong with me?* To think inappropriate thoughts.

Maybe it was better to lean toward friendship. Was choosing a new friend wrong? What about her personal desires. What about love? It was too soon to think about love, but she needed to consider her actions before Taylor wasn't a patient any longer. He would be released from hospital soon.

What about her love life? *My love life.* She hadn't accepted a date, a boyfriend or so much as a sweet kiss in what seemed like forever. What if Taylor was the man she'd been searching for? What if he chanced to be her fish in the ocean? He could as easily be the shark to gnaw at her heart. She groaned and said aloud, "What do I do?"

Sarah needed advice from someone she could trust, and she wasn't ready to talk her family. She grabbed her cell phone and called one of her best friends. Claire answered on the third ring. "Hi, Sarah. It's been a while since we've talked. How are you?"

"Well, it's been one of those days and the day hasn't begun yet," Sarah said, her tone subdued.

"You sound upset. Is everything okay?"

No point in holding the emotion inside. "I've met someone," Sarah said. "There's only one problem…" Her face puckered like she'd bitten into a lemon.

"Okay. This isn't a courtesy call," Claire replied. "You need support. How can I help?"

Sarah sighed. "I admit it; I need advice. His name is Taylor and he's Australian. He has the most beautiful blue eyes I've ever seen. A color that reminds me of the ocean. When he speaks, there's softness in his voice, comfort in his words, which compel me."

"He sounds like a dream. You're not dreaming, are you?" Claire laughed. "But seriously, when did you find the time to meet someone? You're busy. You're always at the hospital."

"Well, actually…"

"Wait a minute," Claire said, her voice rising, "does this potential flame have anything to do with a patient?"

"Maybe." Sarah nibbled at her lip, her brow wrinkled, and her flat sounding voice didn't improve her circumstances. A puff of laughter chortled from the receiver. "Claire, does my situation amuse you?"

"I'm sorry. I'm trying to be sensitive, but the news surprises me." Claire cleared her throat. "Okay, so you've met someone who happens to be your patient. Tell me, is dating a patient a crime?"

"Oh my," Sarah said, moaning, negotiating guilt for having these sensual thoughts. "You don't understand.

Ethically, morally, it's wrong. I need to think about my job, my responsibilities."

"The job that's digging you an early grave?"

"I work on a trauma unit. People's lives are at stake."

"No excuses, my friend. Your life matters, too. What you need is a viewpoint that puts you first," Claire said pointedly. "The last time we talked, you told me you were lonely."

"Sure, but what does loneliness have to do with a relationship?"

"Everything."

Sarah sighed. This conversation was not helping. "Taylor wants to add me as a friend on Facebook. He wants to give me his phone number. I've already compromised the code of conduct by calling his mother."

"What? You talked to his mother?" Claire said, sounding surprised. "Sounds like you're in deep, honey. Why would you do such a thing? That's weird."

Sarah rose from her chair and paced in front of the couch. Now she knew she'd made a mistake. "Someone needed to tell Mrs. Quinn her son had been hurt."

"Hmm, Sarah Quinn. Has a nice *ring* to it."

"Claire! Seriously."

"Okay, okay. But why can't the man call his own mother? This could be a warning sign. He could become your patient for life, so…before I give a yes or a no, let's return to the beginning. Why are you attracted to this Australian in the first place?"

"I didn't say I was attracted."

"You don't have to, Sarah. You're stalling. You wouldn't be considering a new Facebook friend or agreeing to a man's number if you were not attracted to something more than his eyes."

Sarah swallowed. Taylor captivated her, though she wasn't sure exactly why. His charisma? His charm? The way he spoke her name as if she mattered more than his discomfort. An outlandish thought. Taylor loved snowboarding, *not* Sarah Evans.

"Sarah, how long have you known this patient?"

"Only one day," she whispered, gritting her teeth. She suspected this news would come across in the worst way.

"One day?" Claire laughed again, expressing shock. "Are you serious?"

Sarah sighed. "Ah…yes."

"Well, what do you expect me to say? Every woman wants to make a connection."

"I want a boyfriend. I'm tired of being lonely. I want more than my job, more than trauma patients. Running from room to room, from one disgruntled patient to another patient's broken heart. I want…"

"I get it. You don't have to convince me. Add him as a friend."

Sarah sat. "Really? Do you think I should?"

"Why not? What could it hurt? If you don't like what he posts or the way he responds to your comments, you can always unfollow or unfriend him."

"What about the phone number?"

"I wouldn't. That's a personal connection and might be taking it a step too far, after all, you've only known him for one day," Claire said. "And I hate to mention it, but you've been down this road before."

"David," Sarah said, gagging. He'd only offered heartache.

Claire growled. "A controlling jerk. Bradley wasn't much better."

Sarah shook her head, not wanting to concern herself with past boyfriends. The past stays in the past and was best left there. Best to go with gut instincts.

"I'm adding him as a friend."

"Great. I hope he's the prince charming you've been searching for," Claire said. "I'm sorry, I have to go. Peter's testing a new recipe."

"Wait…" Sarah said, surprised, "Peter's at the bakery? I thought he was constructing a change room at the ocean house."

Claire giggled. "The rise in lumber prices put the project on hold."

"There's always something to dampen the spirits."

"Yes, well, seriously…don't be afraid to take a chance, to risk everything, including your job. You, my friend, deserve happiness. It can't be found without effort, without taking a chance."

"Thank you for stating the facts, Claire."

"Good luck with your Australian. I hope this, he—is compatible with you."

"Me, too."

"Sarah," Claire said, her voice sounding serious, "I need to press this point; you deserve happiness. Happiness doesn't come without taking risks."

"Thank you, Claire."

HOLDING HER CELL PHONE, Sarah opened her Facebook App and wrote 'Taylor Quinn' in the search box. When she pressed enter, a few people populated. She found Taylor's profile right away. Her index finger hovered above his name. Should she message Taylor? Add him as a friend?

After the conversation with Claire, Sarah was still uncertain. He was a stranger, but everyone was a stranger when they first met.

"Darn it." Sarah pressed the Add Friend button. She sighed, having made the decision.

Minutes later, Taylor accepted her friend request. She gasped loudly.

Her Messenger App pinged: "Thanks for adding me. You won't regret it."

Excitement overwhelmed her, causing her mind to spin. She didn't understand what this decision meant, for her, for him, yet it intrigued her to find out.

"I hope not," Sarah wrote, typing, "but having you as a Facebook friend feels weird."

"Doesn't to me. It's an unexpected and happy turn of events."

"You think so? We're practically strangers."

"Let's get to know each other. What's your favorite color?"

"That's easy. Orange. What's yours?"

"Blue," Taylor replied. "The color of the ocean."

"I should have known. What's your favorite food?" Sarah asked.

"Fish and chips, English style, served on newspaper."

"How are you today? What's your pain level?"

"A three. Discomfort beneath the ribs. My strength would be greatly improved if my favorite nurse was here."

Sarah nibbled at her lip, questioning if she'd made the right decision. She chose to stop worrying about her job for once and put herself first. "I work the early shift on Monday."

Sarah watched the typing awareness indicator vibrating for several seconds. She waited patiently, wondering what Taylor was writing. After the pause, he said, "Can't wait to see you. Thanks for adding me as a friend. I didn't think you would. Don't take this the wrong way, but there's something special about you."

"I bet you whisper sweet nothings to all the girls."

"Only the ones who matter. I knew you were special from the first moment we met. I'm excited to learn more about you."

"I hope you won't be disappointed in what you find," Sarah replied honestly. "Good night, Taylor, get some rest. I'm off tomorrow, but I'll see you the next day."

"Can't wait. Looking forward to it."

Sarah placed her phone on the side table and moved to the couch. She turned on the TV and chose a news channel from the lineup, but had difficulty focusing on the anchor's commentary. She thought about Taylor and this new relationship, forcing ethical values and negative thoughts concerning her decision to the farthest reaches of her mind. Eventually, she reclined, laying her head on a pillow. She grabbed her phone again and searched for Taylor's profile on Facebook, then reviewed his many photos.

Oh my…he's already liked a few of my posts.

Sarah scrolled through Taylor's profile, viewing a few

photos from Banff Sunshine Village ski and snowboard resort and other photos from Australia.

He seemed happy on the snowboard. The photo must have been taken before the accident. How sad his injury had ended the snowboarding aspirations.

Sarah scrolled through his timeline. He presented well in a business suit. Sarah wondered about his job profession.

Manly Beach? Taylor stood on the sand holding a surfboard. Ocean spray trickled from his wavy hair; his sun-bronzed skin glistened with seawater. Sarah scrutinized every part of his physical appearance. He looked great in board shorts and the surfboard impressed her, too. The backdrop in the distance, a blue ocean with waves rolling to shore, she'd love to experience this seaside, too.

CHAPTER FIVE

The beginning of a new work week, Sarah stood near Taylor's room, watching him eat breakfast. He held a piece of whole wheat toast, the bread smeared with butter and raspberry jam. It coated his fingers and one corner of his mouth. She swallowed, drawn by personal desires to the sweetness on his lips while trying to read his mood.

What did she desire, to suck his fingers, lick his lips or kiss him? When Taylor frowned and placed the partially eaten toast on his plate, her sentiment shifted to one of concern, one motivated by her knowledge of care: nursing.

Taylor seemed upset. *Why?*

"Good morning, Facebook friend," Sarah said, entering the room. "How are you?"

"Hi, Sarah," Taylor replied, his tone solemn and quiet. "I'm fine."

"Why the sour face? Are you upset, or are you in pain?"

"No pain, my health is improving. I'm better, stronger every day, but I can't stop thinking about the accident." He shook his head. "I had this perfect plan, an excellent snowboarding adventure setup, but everything's ruined. I'm not sure what to do. There's too much to think about, to resolve." He sighed, deflating like a balloon. "I had to resign from my job."

Sarah stepped closer. "Where were you employed?"

Taylor looked at the hospital window. "Banff Sunshine Village. The job came with perks, responsibilities, too." He gazed at her, sorrow diminishing the light in his eyes. "I'm sorry, Sarah. I shouldn't be dumping on you. You're not here to listen to my sad stories."

"It's okay, I see you're hurting." But gratefully, only in an emotional way. "Do you want to talk about it?"

"Not really. I know you're busy."

Sarah grasped a chair, pulled it close to the bed and sat. "I've heard Sunshine has a lot of pluses. What will you miss the most?"

"Honestly, the season's pass."

"You've probably been reminded of what you've lost because of the accident."

He looked at her, studying her in a thoughtful way. "You're perceptive."

"It's not difficult to grasp. The disappointment…I get losing something important before you have a chance to enjoy it. Taylor," Sarah said, appealing for sensitivity, "no one can return what's been lost, but it may be helpful to appreciate what you've gained."

"Hmm," he said, giving her the impression she'd asked a pointless question. "What have I gained besides a ruptured spleen and a punch in the gut to go along with it?"

Depression. Acknowledging his state of mind, Sarah didn't speak for the span of several seconds. In her life, she tried to have a positive view when presented with difficult situations, and in her opinion, the accident yielded an obvious benefit; friendship with someone Taylor would never have known if not for the accident. Yet she wouldn't acknowledge the benefits or even their *new* relationship as Taylor wasn't ready for friendlier prospects. *Uh-oh.* Maybe he wasn't as serious about their relationship as she'd hoped. He was depressed, grieving. His focus should be on recovery and overcoming the injury. *Not her.*

"Taylor, may I ask, did you only come to this country to snowboard? Or were there other places you wanted to discover?"

"Pubs, to enjoy a cool one." He gaped, looking at her seriously.

"You'll have to explain that to me. What's a cool one?"

"A coldie, a pint of lager," Taylor said.

"Oh…a beer," Sarah replied, giving a brief laugh. "We label 'cool ones' beer in Canada."

Taylor shook his head. "A beer, then. Look, I planned my trip around snowboarding. A working vacation seemed like the best way to experience winter sports."

"I hope this doesn't come off the wrong way, but your viewpoint seems short-sighted."

Taylor frowned. She'd clearly struck a nerve. He leaned backward, studying her as if she had two heads. "What did you mean?" Oh no, he looked upset. She'd turned sorrow into anger.

"I mean," Sarah said, choosing her words carefully, there's

more to experience in the mountains than one ski resort. There are other places to explore."

Taylor didn't respond. He was clearly in a funk and probably wasn't ready to consider other options.

"What are your plans after you're released from hospital?" Sarah asked, worrying what Taylor might say. "Will you return to Australia?"

"It's on my mind. I may have no other choice," Taylor said in a non-committal way. "My belongings are still at Sunshine. I need to retrieve them. How do I accomplish it? I don't have a vehicle here."

"You could rent one."

"I could, but Australians drive on the opposite side of the motorway. I'm not sure I have the energy or the know-how to tackle driving on the right-hand side."

Motorway? Must be an Australian term.

Sarah hoped she wouldn't regret the suggestion. "I could take you," Sarah said, offering Taylor a half-smile. "I haven't been to the mountains in a while. It could be fun." It could be the opportunity they needed to forge a relationship. They had to start somewhere.

"You'd take me to the hill?" His face brightened slightly. "A generous offer, but I don't want to inconvenience you."

"Is there anyone else who can help?"

"No," he said, shaking his head. "There's no one. I don't have friends or family here."

"How sad." Sarah's heart constricted at the news. Taylor wasn't a lost puppy who needed coddling, he was simply a nice guy facing an inconvenient situation. Why shouldn't she help him? She was a Calgarian first for heaven's sake and this city had a reputation of welcoming its visitors. "Well, that's not exactly true since we became Facebook friends last night."

"Sarah…" Taylor spoke her name gently, sweetly. The action endeared her to him.

"It's okay." She leaned forward and patted his hand. "After all, I promised your mother I'd do my best to care for you." Sarah rose from the chair, her heartstrings buoying her spirits. "Let's make a day of it. I can't return what's been lost, but maybe I can help you find something new."

"You're a kind person."

Taylor became emotional. Though he didn't succumb to tears, she could see the liquid forming in the corners of his eyes, like a dam's water level rising, tears threatened to release. The muscles bunched beneath his eyes, twitching. His face wrinkled, but he didn't lose control. She ached for him in that moment.

"I'm doing my job."

"Your kindness extends *way* beyond work responsibilities." Taylor shifted on the bed. "I see what you're offering. I knew you were special. You're not just another pretty face. There's substance behind your smile. It's unbelievable to find one special person in this country who's willing to help."

Had he said she was pretty? "Taylor, do you have a place to stay? Where will you go after you're released? I mean, you've lost your job, your lodging."

He shook his head. He picked at his fingers. "That's another worry. I'm thinking about traveling home, but for now, I suppose a hotel." He looked at her, the same emotion darkening his eyes. "I can't burden my only friend."

Sarah couldn't bear the thought of Taylor leaving the country. She wasn't ready to say goodbye.

"I want to help." Sarah glanced at the doorway to ensure no one was listening. "What if you stayed at my place?"

"It wouldn't be appropriate. I mean staying with you would be great, but I can't impose."

Sarah leaned in close and acted in an unfamiliar manner. She grasped his shoulder and looked at his beautiful blue eyes. "You're hurt. You're a traveler in a foreign country with no one to rely on. I'm concerned for you. You need to stay somewhere, why not stay with me?"

"I'm a foreigner. You hardly know me and I don't want to burden you." The liquid pooled in his eyes. The emotion, the helplessness gave her the courage to push forward with her personal desires, to help a man from a foreign country.

"You won't be imposing, but if it bothers you, I can charge rent."

"I'll pay it, gladly." A smile brightened Taylor's face. He wiped his eyes.

"It's decided then. You'll stay with me."

Taylor took a deep cleansing breath. He smiled slightly. "Thank you. I suppose I will."

Sarah was glad to help. Patients sometimes required additional measures to mend their wounds, and offering hope had a way of lifting one's spirits. Though she'd never administered optimism in this way before, let alone put forward such an offer to a patient.

Patient? The guilt blossomed in her heart like a budding flower, but she concealed the feelings as best she could. *Stop it, Sarah. Stop seeing Taylor as a patient. He's more than an injured soul, he's my friend.*

Sarah hoped she wouldn't regret this decision.

AFTER SARAH LEFT THE ROOM, Taylor knew he couldn't put off calling his mother any longer. He reached for his cell phone, opened the Skype application, and wasn't surprised to find his mom online even with the time difference. His mother cared deeply for her family and offered her support no matter what crisis befell them. She'd probably been watching for him to come online from the moment Sarah told her about his injury. He should have called sooner.

Taylor initiated the call and his mother answered. When his mother was visible on the screen, his gut twisted. She'd clearly been worried, her eyes lackluster, shrouded with gray. She probably hadn't slept since hearing the news. Taylor wished he'd never been hurt, wished he'd called sooner.

"Taylor," she said, her voice soft, breaking. "What happened?"

"Ah, Mom, it's like the time my foot slipped, and I fell out of the gum tree. You warned me not to climb higher. I should have taken your advice. The mountain..." Taylor sighed, the accident playing in his mind like a movie. "The run challenged my abilities. I fell."

"I'm sorry, Taylor. You were set on having a grand adventure. Knowing you, you're missing the fun."

"I'm disappointed. The pain is lessening."

"A nurse called. She said you ruptured your spleen. Is that true?"

Mom wiped a tear from the corner of her eye. "Don't cry, Mom. It's okay, I'm okay. The doctors and nurses have provided excellent care. I'm healing. I'll be well enough to leave the hospital in a day or two."

Taylor's dad appeared on the screen. Though he tried to conceal his concern, the look in his eyes exposed a serious, controlled demeanor. "You okay, son?"

"Yeah, Dad, but it's not all sad news. You warned me about socializing with the ladies before I left home, and you won't believe this, but your premonition has come true. I met someone."

Humor twinkled in his father's eyes; a light Taylor had appreciated since boyhood days. Dad shook his head, but he kept on smiling. "You haven't been in the country that long." He laughed. "You take after your father with your smart moves."

"Dad…It's not the same as ballroom dancing."

"Where did you meet her? At the mountain or at the hospital?"

His mother's eyes filled with merriment. "It's the nurse."

Taylor couldn't keep anything from his mother. "Yeah, Mom, the nurse. The only sunshine to come from this accident."

"Wonderful, we're happy for you," his father replied. "You said you'd be released soon. Where will you stay?" The question disguised uneasiness, but Taylor understood the concern.

"Sarah's invited me to stay with her. It's a generous

invitation given our recent friendship, but the arrangement rubs me the wrong way. I don't want to impose. What should I do? Should I accept?"

"Really?" Mother asked. "Taylor, is that a good idea? Maybe it's best to come home."

Taylor grasped his side, feeling the familiar ache. He might need to travel, but not until his strength returned. Not until he better understood the bond between him and Sarah.

"I can't come home, not right now. I need to recover, but even if I was ready, there's something about Sarah. A feeling, a connection. I need to determine what it is and the only way to do that is to spend time with Sarah."

"Take your time," his father said. "We're not with you; you have to use your best judgment."

"I appreciate the support."

His mother sighed. "I suppose if you have to stay with someone while recovering, who better than a nurse?"

Who better than Sarah? No one held his attention more than Sarah, but Taylor didn't disclose this. "Good call, Mom. Have you told Adam?"

"Yes, your sister as well."

"What did Adam say?"

"You take after your big brother."

CHAPTER SIX

Days later, Taylor discharged from the hospital at noon. As a new patient needed his room, Sarah met him in the waiting area at the end of her shift, shortly after three p.m. The man sitting on the jade leather chair appeared healthier now that he wasn't wearing a bland hospital gown. His cheeks were rosy, his eyes brighter, and he seemed composed and relaxed in a marine blue sweater and distressed jeans. Sarah paused in the corridor to admire his broad shoulders and chest that tapered to a slim waistline.

When he caught her staring, Taylor gave her a wry smile. Sarah moved closer, pushing the wheelchair.

"Nope. No way…I'm not sitting in that chair."

Sarah stopped near him and applied the brake. "Hey, only the best rides for our best patients. But even if the chair wasn't routine, it's a hike to my car. You'll be more comfortable."

"I'm not an invalid."

"No one said you were."

"Sarah…" He complained, murmuring. "I'm fine. I can

walk." He appealed to her like a playful puppy dog, making her heart swoon and earning the additional animal magnetism of wanting to scratch behind his ears or run her fingers through his messy hair.

"Don't be difficult." Sarah's brows rose while shifting the foot plates out of the way. "If distraction helps, pretend you're on the ski lift, riding toward one incredible run."

"You're enjoying this too much," Taylor said, giving a slight laugh, "have it your way." He rose from the chair and settled in the wheelchair.

Sarah shifted the foot plates into place. "Are you ready to leave this place?"

"I was ready a week ago." He tapped the armrest. "Be careful, don't round the corners too fast."

Sarah smiled while unlocking the brake, soon shifting the chair into motion. "I thought you liked going fast."

"Depends on where I'm riding."

Sarah didn't say much while wheeling Taylor out of the waiting room and into the hallway. She pushed the wheelchair along the hospital corridor, moving toward the nursing station. She swallowed her anxiety as she drew closer. The head nurse looked up from her work and peered at Sarah quizzically. *What am I doing?* Sarah had to get through this momentary discomfort and stop worrying about her colleagues judging her actions. Their criticism didn't matter. She tried to act in control, as if escorting Taylor from the unit was completely natural. In a calm and controlled voice, she said, "Good night, Kris."

Kris's eyebrows rose. "Good night, Sarah."

Judgment—Assessment in piercing eyes and a shrewd face

that wrinkled with curiosity. A questioning mien that inquired *'why'* she helped a patient leave the unit after her shift had ended. Suddenly, she didn't care what colleagues thought. Why should she? This was her life to live, her decision to make. If it was a misstep to share a relationship with Taylor, then it was her slipup and none of Kris's business.

Kris shook her head. "All the best to you, Taylor."

Taylor waved and they carried on, leaving the unit. They were soon on the elevator, and before Sarah knew it, she was wheeling Taylor toward her silver Jetta. Once there, she engaged the brake and helped Taylor stand. She unlocked the car door and Taylor entered the vehicle on the passenger side. She could tell by his pinched expression he was experiencing discomfort, but this was expected. He was healing. He needed care, rest and relaxation, which helped her appreciate she'd made the right decision. She could help him with the medical needs.

Sarah took the wheelchair to the elevator and then returned to her car, to Taylor. She sat in the driver's seat and placed the key in the ignition, imparting a dreamy look. "Are you ready? Is your seatbelt fastened?" Her girlish heart empathized with the man reclining in her car, and honestly, she looked forward to exploring the emotions passing between them.

He nodded, massaging the belt. "I miss my Subaru. It feels strange sitting on the right-hand side. The passenger seat is located on the left side of an Australian vehicle."

"Really? Seems odd."

"Maybe you'll experience the Aussie side of the car one

day. Then, I'd be the driver. I'd take you places. Scenic beaches, a koala bear petting zoo, a crocodile farm if you're adventurous," he said, snickering.

"I'm not afraid of crocodiles."

"You wouldn't like the freshies, but don't worry about them, we don't have crocs in Sydney. They lurk in the northern rivers and beaches."

Sarah shook her head, placing her foot on the brake. "Don't take this the wrong way, but when I travel to Australia, I'll start my trip in Sydney."

"Seriously, would you travel down under?"

Sarah glanced at Taylor while turning the key in the ignition. The engine fired to life. "Yes, I would. I've always wanted to visit Australia." She checked the rearview mirror and backed out of the stall.

"You could stay with me."

Sarah smiled, driving toward the parking structure's exit. "That's a great offer. I'll have to think about it."

Sarah glanced at Taylor. It gave her a peculiar yet remarkable feeling to think their relationship could extend beyond her country. Taylor suggested a woman he barely knew was welcome to visit him in Sydney. The meaning behind the offer compelled her head to spin.

What would traveling to Sydney imply?

She needed a break from work. A partner would be appreciated, too. Most men wouldn't risk making their intentions clear unless the prospect of a deeper bond stimulated the rationale, and as she glanced at Taylor a second time, she wondered whether the real strategy proposed friendlier ties.

Taylor's eyebrows rose as if he was reading her thoughts. "Are you sure about this, Sarah?"

"About what?"

"It's not too late to take me to a hotel. I wouldn't judge you for changing the plan."

Sarah shoulder checked and then turned right onto the laneway. "No worries, Taylor. It's fine."

"If you're comfortable with the idea, then why are you so quiet?"

Sarah glanced at Taylor thoughtfully, not sure of anything other than the sense some risks were worth taking while returning her attention to the road. She applied pressure to the brake at the juncture of Hospital Drive, thinking. Doubt shouldn't intrude on happy thoughts. Taylor Quinn was welcome in her life, in her car and her condo.

She signaled right and drove in that direction. "No worries, Taylor." She purposely used the Australian phrase. "If you're sensing doubt, from me or from yourself, well…that's understandable. It's not every day a nurse puts herself in an awkward situation by taking her patient home." It went against everything she'd been taught, but some rules were meant to be broken.

"Have you done this before?" Taylor asked, amusement creasing his face. "Taken a patient home for a *special* round of care?"

"Ah," Sarah said, frowning. "This is out of character for me. I've taken animals home. A lost dog, a mewling kitten, but a patient… Honestly? Never. Consider yourself a special case."

"I get it. I understand why you're uncomfortable."

Sarah glanced at Taylor. "I'm fine. I'm satisfied with the arrangement."

"Are you? Cause you're quiet. You're tapping the steering wheel like a drill sergeant."

Sarah immediately stopped.

"Look, to ensure we're in agreement, if I were you, I'd be uncertain as well. If it makes you more at ease, I'm not a hunter and I don't carry weapons. I don't own a gun; can't imagine carrying a gun. All I ask is that you restrict judgment until you have a clear idea of who I am. If it helps, I've been known to cuddle the odd teddy bear."

He had the build of a teddy bear, especially while wearing the thick sweater. Sarah reflected on broad shoulders, strong arms, arms that could hold her, hug her, and sitting this close the scent of woodsy aftershave filled the car. She caressed the steering wheel, licking her lips. "Do you own a teddy bear?"

"Maybe."

"That's non-committal. I have nieces and nephews. They like plush."

"We're getting to know each other, so you must have questions about my character. Let me assure you, I have morals, values I gained from my parents. I'm an honest, dependable guy. I respect people's rights."

"I appreciate what you're trying to say."

"Sarah, I'm picky when it comes to the opposite sex. I'm single. I've been searching, but I've never found a like-minded partner. But you... You don't seem like the type of woman who'd bring strange men into your life or into your home."

Sarah shook her head. "You might be from Australia but

you're not unlike Canadian men. I certainly would never label you as strange."

"It's the accent you're attracted to." Taylor grinned, winking. "I'd never hurt you and I suspect you'd never hurt me." Nope. She'd never hurt him, and he was right. The accent appealed to her in indescribable ways.

"I'm a nurse. Hurting patients goes against the job description." Sarah snickered under her breath while making a turn. "Hurt you? Not after nursing you back to health."

"Thank you for your care," Taylor said, his tone soft and grateful.

Sarah glanced at Taylor. "Whatever you're trying to say, it's working. I'm more comfortable with my decision. I appreciate your honesty."

"You're welcome."

Sarah was a nurse, but with her busy, hectic life, some days she wondered why she still worked in the profession. She had higher plans, furtive goals. Someday she wanted to pursue health systems, assisting organizations, people and actions, with a primary intent to promote, restore and maintain health. Maybe take further education to manage health-improving activities.

"Can I ask you a question?" Sarah asked.

"Ask me anything."

Sarah took a deep breath while approaching the Trans-Canada Highway, the last leg of the journey home. "Are you attracted to me?" She gritted her teeth, waiting for his response, wondering why she raised the subject.

"Sarah…"

"No, seriously, I want to know."

He blushed. "Yes, of course, what healthy male wouldn't be attracted to your charm?" Taylor asked, his tone subdued. "Honestly, from the moment you first touched me."

She glanced at him, curious for an explanation. "How so?"

"How do I explain that first sighting? The first touch?" He looked through the car window as if remembering. "You were gentle. You may have rushed from room to room and patient to patient, but when you were with me, you gave me your complete attention." He looked at her again. "You were kind."

"That's my job, my responsibility as a nurse. I try to deliver the best healthcare to my patients."

"You're modest. I haven't been around a lot of nurses, but I have a good rapport with people. My previous job as a mortgage broker put me in contact with many clients. Some of them astute, and others too business savvy and not worth the investment of my time." He touched her hand, her fingers, stroking in a sensual way. "But you, you're a kind, considerate person. I'm aware of this because…"

"Because why? Finish what you were going to say."

"You touched me. In ways difficult to describe. You not only nursed me but also gave me a place to stay. Who offers that kind of hope?" The sudden silence in the car urged a response, but Sarah waited patiently for Taylor to speak. "You're a woman and I'm a man, brass tacks and sweet perfume. Not every woman opens her heart, giving a guy a place to stay. We're new. We're strangers, but here I am, in your car and in your life."

"I can't believe you're here." It was like she'd willed it to happen, willed Taylor into her life and somehow, he was here.

"Sarah, you're special."

She'd heard such praise from her parents, but never from someone of the opposite sex. She'd been waiting her entire life for a man to recognize her special traits. The comment gave her pleasant feelings of happiness. She blushed. "Thank you. That's kind of you."

"I mean it." He touched her thigh, a skimming touch that sent vibrations from her thigh to her heart.

"I believe you." Sarah exited the highway and drove onto Bowfort Road. "What's happening between us, Taylor?"

"I'm not sure, but I'm keen to find out."

CHAPTER SEVEN

"You have a beautiful home," Taylor said, his tone subdued, his posture unyielding. He stood near the picture window with his hands dangling near his thighs, his fingers fidgety while studying the mountains in the distance. "That's one spectacular view."

"Many of my friends have stood where you're standing, watching the sun as it sets behind the mountain range. I knew you'd appreciate it."

Beyond the condo, the extraordinary light show accentuated wonder. Spectacular shades of orange and flowery pink streaked across the twilight sky, but the man standing in front of the window with the last vestiges of light softening his eyes, appealed to Sarah more than the distant panorama. She concentrated on Taylor, not believing she'd had the courage to invite him into her home. Taylor Quinn was her secret. She hadn't told her parents about bringing him into her life and into her home, hadn't told her friends. They'd judge her. Opposing opinions might be necessary in some situations, but in this case, Sarah wasn't ready to face reality.

This decision rationalized what could be. Taylor might be the one.

While waiting for the kettle to boil, Sarah glanced at Taylor frequently, feeling this pull, this desire to lessen the distance between them. In this moment, his fragile medical needs were not apparent, but rather his misery; the accident, the loss, the regret, the mountains: the place where he had chosen to pursue a sporting activity. He likely aspired to return to an adventurous life, perhaps wanting more than collecting belongings from the ski hill, but snowboarding wasn't possible with his injury. He hadn't said much about the season being cut short, but the disappointment shadowed his eyes, stiff posture, and tight lips.

I want to touch those lips.

She wanted to help him relax, to take him for a drive, to the mountains he admired, to complete unfinished goals, to return his smile by exploring uncharted options.

Sometimes, life didn't play fair, but the simple act of living made possible each person's turning points. Sarah suspected unknown adventures lay ahead. How could she help Taylor see this?

"I'VE ALWAYS ADMIRED the mountain view," Sarah finally said, choosing to focus on the positive. "Besides the proximity to the hospital, I bought this condo because of the mountains in the distance." She paused, struggling with what to say. "There's another benefit to living in this community…the proximity to the Bow River and its walking paths. When I'm in a bad mood, I go to the river's edge."

"I understand, Sarah, but please don't worry. I'm fine." He sighed, rubbing his neck. "Do you like the paths, the water?"

Sarah did not comment on his grief. "I love the water. There's a park near the river. Sometimes when I'm stressed, I grab a coffee from Tim Hortons. It's a popular restaurant in Canada, all the locals go there. I sit on a bench. I watch rolling water, the current flowing downstream."

He faced her, placing his hands in his pant pockets. "Sounds beautiful."

"You'd love it," Sarah said. "I can't compare the river to an ocean. Though the sunlight sparkles on the water's surface like millions of tiny diamonds. And the sound of running water, or the effervescence in the air…I breathe deeply, filling my lungs with peace."

"Peace. I could use some of that." Sarah closed her eyes. "I wish it was summer, everything's better when the sun warms my skin."

Sarah imagined herself near the shoreline. *I need the river. I need peace. Love—*

Taylor reached for a chair and sat at the table. When she opened her eyes, he was staring at her, studying her in a curious manner while stroking the table. He seemed calmer. "Do you only stare at the water? Life is more exciting when experiencing it."

"Not at this time of year," Sarah said. "I'm grateful the condo came with a garage so I could escape the weather at the end of the day. Winter can be harsh, driving through snow difficult, and the water's bloody cold right now. The shoreline is frozen. But in the heat of summer, I've dipped my toes in the water."

Taylor raised his hand. "No judgment here, but do you *ever* wade into the water? Can you swim? Reminds me of the ocean and my surfboard. Nothing compares to riding the waves. Before the ocean's upsurge there's the pull of the water, the lure of the sea. The swell boosts me upward, and then hopefully, takes me for a long-drawn-out ride."

"Sounds scary."

"There's no better feeling. The momentum captures your breath." Taylor breathed deeply. "Rain or shine, it's a peaceful place. When I'm surfing, I have *no worries*. No conversation to frustrate me or cause upset, nothing distracts from the vibe when I'm a lone surfer floating on the water."

"A place where worries have no hold."

Taylor smiled. "Yes, that's right. There's a reason Aussies coined the phrase: 'No Worries.' I'm certain whoever put the saying into words said it because of the ocean."

"I like that expression."

"We could go to your river, wouldn't matter to me if the sky hung heavy with rain or the banks glistened with snow. I want to experience what peace means to you."

Sarah nodded, smiling slightly, appreciating that Taylor respected her point of view. Somewhere in this sadness and thought they'd made a connection. "You've given me a lot to consider."

When the kettle boiled and steam spiraled into the air, Sarah grabbed two mugs from the cupboard and placed a tea bag in each. She poured boiling water into the mugs and handed Taylor the drink. She sat near him, holding her mug with both hands. "I'm not sure if I'd be brave enough to surf. Seeing patients with various injuries has made me cautious, and maybe too careful."

"Aha…so that's it."

"Partly." Sarah sipped her tea.

"Don't let other people's accidents prevent you from experiencing life."

"Taylor, it's one thing to stare at the ocean, quite another to wade through the waves and stand on a board. I've never surfed. What could happen to me while waiting for the curl?"

His eyebrows rose. He grinned. "Nothing happens until you face your fears. You could have an amazing ride while sitting on the board boogie style, or…you could wipe out. But at least you're face-planting in the water, not the snow." He looked at her in a tangible way.

"Point well taken." Though it wasn't water sports motivating Sarah to daydream. She imagined Taylor, his body lean, strong, wearing a wet suit and straddling or standing on a surfboard, floating on the waves. "Does the ocean *ever* frighten you?"

"It's a crabby beast on stormy days," Taylor said with a shrug. "Best to avoid the waves when the water's rough, but on good days…I'm one with the water. Life surges through me in the best way possible when the wave comes."

"Have you been hurt while pursuing this, surfing?"

"Huh." Taylor gave a brief laugh. "Not like on my snowboard, that was traumatic, but you know," Taylor said, massaging his side, "water is much easier to wipe out on and I've never been attacked by a shark."

Sarah's eyes widened while picturing massive jaws with

razor-sharp teeth. She hadn't considered dangerous sealife. "I was referring to the height of the waves," she gasped, "not sharks. Oh. My. God. I'm never swimming in your ocean."

Taylor laughed, downplaying her reaction. "It's not that terrifying. I haven't been eaten, not yet."

"Don't think it." Sarah shook her head. "Once, I watched a surfing competition in Hawaii on the northern shore. The waves were monstrous. High. The curls amazed me. The surfing mind-blowing to watch, but it must have been scary for the riders."

"It's a sport. Surfers are trained professionals, but the waves can be heavy, gnarly in Hawaii. No one goes into the pipe without training."

Sarah sipped her tea, amazed by his turn of phrase. "I couldn't do it."

He studied her in a contemplative way. He reached across the table but didn't touch her. "Yes, you could. If you wanted to experience an activity more momentous than a hard bench." His eyes brightened. "If you have not learned to swim, I could teach you."

"I can swim."

Sarah contemplated Taylor's teaching skills, wondering if she'd be able to balance on a board let alone facing the unfamiliar motion of waves. "Surfing sounds like it would be a stimulating and terrifying experience. I'd probably be better suited to searching for shells on the beach."

"Would you be willing to try?"

He leaned backward, reached for his mug, and took a sip of tea, all the while studying her, contemplating something she couldn't name. What was he thinking? Feeling? He studied her in an inquisitive manner, expressing with one long stare needs that could not be defined. When he probed her like a potential cohort, 'a friend or something more?', no way was she giving a no answer.

"If you were the teacher offering lessons—yes, yes, I would."

THEY TALKED FOR OVER AN HOUR. Taylor told Sarah stories about his life in Australia; his previous job, his family, friends, and she did similar. They were vastly different in some ways and curiously similar in others. When the dinner hour drew near, Taylor wanted to experience a Canadian meal and offered to take her out for dinner, but since he was recently released from hospital, Sarah decided they should stay home. She made poutine and smothered the fries with mozzarella cheese and gravy. Cheese curds were an essential ingredient, but she didn't have any in the fridge. They'd experience the authentic version on another occasion.

"Tell me something your friends don't know about you?" Sarah asked, shifting her fries around her plate.

"I can dance."

Sarah's brows lifted in surprise. "Like at a club, or have you taken professional lessons?"

His face wrinkled with amusement. "You don't believe me."

"I didn't say that." Sarah tried to swallow her humor. She wasn't sure why she felt the need to laugh.

He placed his fork on his plate and leaned backward.

"Despite your surprise, some guys *do* take dance lessons." His eyebrows shot upward. "My father…" He strained for patience, raising his hands. "I'm proud of him. I mean, he's a brilliant man, a credit to the engineering profession and a real dance instructor. Although he's retired, he teaches ballroom dancing in his spare time."

"Really?" Now Sarah felt bad. "If I came off as rude…"

"It's all right."

"I'm sorry, Taylor," Sarah said, meaning it. As much as the dancing revelation surprised her, it also heightened the pleasure. Men who could dance were rare and knowing he had this talent encouraged further scrutiny. "What dances are you familiar with?"

Taylor touched his chest and lifted his left arm upward as if his intention might be to escort her onto the dance floor. "The tango, the foxtrot, the Cha Cha Cha…" He winked, shifting his shoulders from side to side. "But for a couple, there's no better dance than the waltz."

A couple? Sarah tried to picture what it would be like to dance with Taylor, his hand holding hers, their fingers entwined, the two of them swaying to the rhythm and moving across the floor like dancers on *So You Think You Can Dance*. She spooned a fry smothered with cheese and gravy into her mouth, her tastebuds waters, desiring Taylor to embrace her. She didn't acknowledge she had taken dance lessons as well.

"Sounds like you have the moves." She flashed him a coy, playful look that gave the impression of teasing.

"Maybe," Taylor said, smiling at first, then placing his fork on the table. "We could give it a go if you're willing. I may not have my father's skill, but I don't mind giving a lesson, if you're interested."

Though Sarah shook her head, curiosity aroused her interest, encouraging her to take their relationship and dance lessons to the next step, but she focused on the obvious. "You're still healing. I don't want you to hurt yourself."

"Hey, waltzing isn't difficult." He shifted his chair away from the table and stood, then extended his left hand. "Will you be my partner?"

"Sure." Why not agree to a lesson? It was too thought-provoking to say no to a dance lesson, so Sarah rose from her chair, came around the table and grasped his hand. His gorgeous blue eyes sparkled with mischief while holding her fingers. But the simple act of touching his skin awakened hidden desires and contributed to a fluttering heart. He stood near her, staring at her, as if he wasn't acquainted with the steps, as if he'd never escorted a woman onto the dance floor let alone taken a lesson.

It was time to initiate the steps.

Should she reveal she knew the routine or let Taylor take the lead? "Now that you have your partner, what comes next?"

"I gather my girl." *His girl?* Taylor pulled her closer to him and placed his right hand slightly above her waist. His touch and the proximity to her, even with her cotton shirt as a barrier, caused sensual awareness to flare to life. Sarah swallowed, reflecting on his curious expression and the way his breathing wisped from his mouth. Though his embrace was slight, his hand hardly touching her waist, she desired his touch, his embrace, and wanted to flirt in a real ballroom.

"Sarah…"

Did he recognize the need flaring between them? Taylor studied her as if he hungered for something more filling than a meal, but then released his handhold. "I'd like to escort you to the dance floor."

"Okay," she said, sighing, stepping backward, "but you're healing, don't move too fast. Be careful."

When Taylor escorted Sarah to the space between the kitchen and the living room, she felt twenty years younger, like she had little experience, in relationships, in dance, like she'd never taken a turn across the floor, but once they were standing on the hardwood, holding hands, facing each other… passion flared to life in his eyes, his beautiful blue eyes.

Taylor breathed deeply. He squeezed her hand and held his position, again. "Before I make a complete fool of myself, have you done this before?"

"I may have," Sarah said, her lips rising to a half-smile, "but not with a dancer from Australia."

"We're starting with a box step. When I step forward with my left foot, you step back with your right. Then it's a simple forward-side-close, or in your case, back-side-close. Ready to try?"

"Yes, let's do it."

"On the count of three," Taylor said, noticeably swallowing, "one, two, three…"

When Taylor stepped forward, his passionate gaze and the slight handhold on her waist teased her senses. She didn't budge, didn't dance, her only need to discover the love shining in his eyes. Taylor stepped forward onto her foot.

Ouch! It hurt. She instinctively shifted away, but her focus and reaction had little to do with discomfort. His masculine appeal and the desire shining in his eyes enticed her.

"I'm sorry," Taylor said, releasing her, wiping his hands on his jeans. "Are my hands warm, sweaty? Am I holding you too tightly?"

"It's all right," Sarah replied, swallowing. "I wasn't ready. Let's try again."

This time when Taylor stepped forward, Sarah stepped backward. They danced in perfect harmony. One, two, three; step touch close. "You've done this before," Taylor said, leading her around the room.

"Yes," Sarah replied, squeezing his fingers. "I've taken dance lessons as well, but I've never had a partner like you." The compliment earned her a smile.

"Ready for the dip?"

"Do you think we should?"

"I've got this." Taylor embraced her and shifted her closer. She welcomed his strength, his hand on the small of her back. She swallowed the desire, gazing at him intently from the simple feeling of being held.

He leaned forward, his self-control and leading role dominating her attention as he came closer to her neck. She nearly swooned when his warm breath fanned her skin, but then a painful grimace pinched his face, stifling the mood. "Taylor…"

He released her, dropping her to the floor.

Shocked and lying on the hardwood, Sarah would have complained, until the moment sheer agony tore across Taylor's face. She disregarded her discomfort and rose from the floor. What had they done? He was still healing. Apparently difficult dance moves shouldn't happen yet.

Taylor clutched his side, moaning, unable to speak.

"Taylor, are you okay?"

He nodded. "My pride is bruised, my ribs as well," he said, wincing. "I'm sorry. I've never let a dancer down like that before."

"No worries," Sarah said, grasping his hand. "No harm was done. I'm okay. Come, sit with me." She led him to the couch. "I never should have agreed to the last step."

"When the moves were taking a good turn across the floor." Taylor shook his head. "It's my fault." His face pinched while sitting. "I don't understand my own limitations."

"It's all right. You've got this." Sarah sat beside Taylor. Pain and anxiety marred his face.

"When will this pain go away?"

Sarah squeezed his hand reassuringly. "You need to be careful while lifting for at least three weeks. Your nurse needs to take better care of you. You're not supposed to lift weight greater than ten pounds. I'm heavier than that," Sarah said with a grimace. "I'll get the pain reliever." Sarah returned to her nurse's role, robbing each of them from sensual heat.

Gratitude washed over him, draining his expression. "Thank you, Sarah."

He was quiet while Sarah retrieved his medication. She nibbled at her lip. "We probably shouldn't dance until you're fully recovered."

He gave an audible sigh. "Are you sure? Everything was fine prior to the dip."

Sarah didn't say much while retrieving a glass of water and

two pills from the Tylenol bottle, but until the dip, she'd known complete bliss. The way he held her, looked at her, the need in his eyes, his hand on the small of her back, the emotion prompted hidden desires to fire between them.

Their romance courted a need she hadn't touched before. Love—

She hoped their relationship would mature into a promising connection.

CHAPTER EIGHT

Mountains soared above them. Evergreens frosted with white pearls standing on either side of the motorway, and higher still on upper ridges where sharp gray rock contrasted sharply with a marine blue sky. It was gorgeous. Taylor observed it all, appreciating the scenery as he had the first time. Though viewing it now encouraged joy as well as sorrow. He frowned, remembering the holiday and the accident that had put a stop to his mountain adventure.

As they drove closer to Banff Sunshine Village, the mishap wasn't any easier to accept. Snowboarding was off limits. In the passenger seat of Sarah's car, Taylor massaged his side. Several days had passed and the ache in his abdomen hadn't eased.

He shook his head, hiding the pain, distracting himself from displeasure by watching the passing scenery or by listening to music on the radio. He glanced at the caring woman in the driver's seat who softened his disappointment.

He studied her sweet face, contemplating qualities equally if not more beautiful than mountain scenery—Sarah.

Without this woman, he'd have nothing to look forward to.

When the song "*Home*" crooned from the radio, Taylor reached for the dial and turned up the volume, eyeing Sarah as if to ask if it was okay.

She nodded.

He whistled the intro of the tune, surprising her with his musical ability.

Sarah's eyebrows rose. She glanced at him momentarily. "Have you heard this song before?" she asked, focusing on the road ahead, holding the steering wheel with both hands.

"It's one of my favorites," Taylor replied.

"Then you'll love this part," she said, singing: "Alabama, Arkansas…I still love my Ma and Pa. Not the way I would love you…"

"Hey," Taylor said, forgetting his troubles, "you have a great voice."

Sarah giggled, a huge smile brightening her face. "It's raw around the edges, but who cares, I love singing this song."

Taylor watched Sarah tapping her fingers against the steering wheel in time to the rhythm. A new appreciation for this woman caused him to smile, too.

Maybe the song prompted her to say, *"Home is wherever there is you…"*

"Me?" he asked, tapping his fingers against the door handle. "I'm flattered."

Sarah blushed, her cheeks blossoming to a light shade of

pink, then looking away as if revealing too much. "When we arrive at the ski resort, where do we go?" Sarah asked.

The sound of Sarah's voice echoing in the car resonated with Taylor while listening to the song on the radio, but he didn't want his actions to make her uncomfortable, so he focused on the view outside the vehicle. "I messaged Luke. Unfortunately, he's working today, or he would have met us at the base. We'll park and take the gondola to the village. I'll pay the fee."

"Are you nervous about returning to the mountain?"

"Honestly, yes. I can't get over the shock. I came here to conquer the hill, to ride through white stuff. It hits home, you know, suffering this defeat."

"It's normal to face regrets, to grieve what's been lost. Anyone in your situation would react in similar ways."

Taylor glanced at Sarah then, really looking at her, her chocolate-brown hair with gold highlights and big brown eyes sparking with interest, kindness, and sympathy for his situation. He'd lost a season of snowboarding, but had he found something else? Had he found his real home, with Sarah? It was too soon to know.

But when she smiled, her eyes sparkling as if sunlight streamed from within, he wanted to dig beneath the surface of their relationship to discover what home they were shaping. "You'd think it would be easy to leave the past behind, but it's not. The accident occupies my mind every day."

"You need to pivot," Sarah said, giving him a firm stare. "It's hard to shift focus after a life-changing event. You came to Canada to snowboard. I'm sure you miss it, especially when we're traveling to Sunshine. Taylor, you're still grieving."

He fingered the door handle, his hand bunched into a fist. "I guess I am."

"No worries," Sarah said, winking, blowing a strand of hair from her eyes, "you'll overcome the disappointment. In time, the pain will lessen."

She'd verbalized the Australian phrase like a pro. That meant a lot to Taylor. He could see she cared. About him? "I appreciate your positive attitude. I'm grateful for your support."

Sarah's professional approach filled Taylor with gratitude. Having had her as his nurse, and now living in her home for the past few days, he knew he was attracted to her. Thinking about this new friendship, his heart grew, the beat increasing simply from looking at her. Something else swelled from time to time, but it was too soon to engage in a physical relationship.

"You know what," Sarah said, sighing, "some days if I didn't laugh, I'd cry."

"I can well imagine, given your occupation." Taylor took a chance and touched her fingers on the steering wheel. He heard her indrawn breath. "You have to expand on that."

She sniffed. "My job comes with good days and bad. Not everyone recovers. Not every patient gets a second chance."

Taylor nodded. "You've seen people die."

Sarah gave an audible sigh.

Taylor stroked her finger then pulled away, not wanting to distract the driver. "It must be terrible facing a life loss, especially with a younger patient. My problems are insignificant when compared to a life lost."

She glanced at him momentarily, frowning. "All endings are difficult to accept, no matter how they happen, but you, you'll get a second chance. You'll snowboard again." Sarah looked at him meaningfully. "We haven't known each other for long, but from everything you've told me, you're not the type to give up without a fight."

Taylor shook his head. "Not usually. Who knows when I'll travel here again. It's a long journey to Canada. The distance between your Canadian Rockies and my Australian ocean…well, there's many miles and countless hours between the two." He hadn't allowed for Sarah's home and his home. Could the two become one?

They looked at each other, equally facing the gravity of what he'd said. Given his injury, Taylor suspected he'd have to leave Canada. He'd researched flight options, knowing sooner or later he must travel to Sydney, and if he did, what then? How could he pursue a relationship with an ocean between him and his love interest? The thought of leaving Sarah caused a tightening in his chest. His heart ached; his head hurt. Traveling home warred with his mind, worrying him more than the dull pain beneath his ribs.

Sarah affected him emotionally and they barely knew each other.

Where was his home? Was it with her? With Sarah?

If they were meant to be a couple, making a home in Canada seemed important, but with the pain beneath his ribs, staying might not be a good idea. Insurance wouldn't cover further expenses. No, he shouldn't go home, not yet. Though leaving might end this interesting, crazy vibe.

Who am I trying to convince?

Taylor looked at Sarah briefly, sensing uneasiness.

When it came to a man's resolve, sometimes decisions were complex. Though he wouldn't abandon this country until answering one all-important question: His home, his life, was it with Sarah Evans?

CHAPTER NINE

When Luke traded his shift, they met for lunch at Mad Trappers Smokehouse near the base of the chairlift. The restaurant imparted a cabin-like atmosphere with rustic log walls and a stone fireplace. It was crowded. Loud. The noise from other guests made it difficult to comprehend Luke and Taylor's conversation. Though the snippets Sarah heard seemed one-sided.

Two friends ignored Taylor's accident or even the recovery while discussing Luke's snowboarding exploits. To some it would have appeared rude, but it gave Sarah an appreciation of their friendship. A chumminess reflected in laid-back conversation paired with laughter and the odd joke.

Sarah could hardly get a word in, but she didn't mind. It entertained her observing a side of Taylor through the lens of Luke.

"Tin Can Alley amazed me. It's cloudy today, but the view from the top: trees topped with snow and fresh powder on the run, man…I flew across it, veering in and out of the trees, feeling more alive than I've felt in years."

When the comment earned Taylor's silence, Luke paused, his face wrinkling in thought. Maybe he'd finally wizened to his insensitivity. "What's wrong? Do my stories upset you or something?"

Taylor didn't answer the question, choosing to sip his beer.

"It does upset you. Man, I'm sorry. Sorrier still you were not riding with me."

"That's all right," Taylor said, shrugging, fingering his beer like a lost child. Sarah watched long slim fingers barely touching the glass, aware of the somber attitude.

Undeterred, Luke expounded his view, voicing concern. "Don't pout, mate, it's not forever. You'll ride again. When will you be ready? Two weeks. Three? We need to finish what we started."

When the two friends stared at each other, each of them waiting for the other to speak, Sarah interjected, "It's a significant injury. Taylor's recovery will take months, not weeks."

"Really, that long? The season will be over by then," Luke said, wincing. His face puckered as if her explanation had given him fake news. He licked his lips in irritation. "That's right, you're the nurse."

Sarah opened her mouth to speak, then didn't. One brief comment reminded her of the risk she'd taken in having a relationship with Taylor. Guilt clouded her thinking, her face flamed, her cheeks colored a bright shade of red.

Embarrassed, she looked at Taylor. He glanced at her momentarily, shaking his head.

"Luke, you're a friend, but please...don't be rude to Sarah. She's a friend, too. I don't know what I would have done without her."

Quiet, Luke leaned backward in his chair and took a swig of beer. *Thank you for the pause.* His rambling diatribe, blathering on and on, had become annoying. Luke's exploits might be exciting for him to share but the snowboarding stories saddened Taylor.

"Hey, I didn't mean to offend you, either of you. It's an upsetting change of affairs."

"I'm the one who was hurt," Taylor said quietly.

Luke raised his hands. "I get it, but you can't blame me for the accident." Luke took a deep breath. "Man, I'm sorry." Now Luke seemed upset. "We came to Canada together. We were supposed to experience the mountains, the snowboarding, the whole mind-bending ride...together. I'm disappointed, too. Who else can I share this with?"

"Hey," Sarah said, appealing for calm, "no one is more upset than Taylor."

Luke pointed at her, grinning, laughing nervously, nudging her arm. "You're blushing." He reached for his beer and took a sip, then gave Taylor a teasing jab. "Maybe *this* worked out better for you. Do you have a thing for this nurse, mate?"

Sarah nearly gagged. She was astonished by his nerve.

Taylor glanced at her. His brows rose upward, his eyes sparkled. "Maybe. Maybe I do." He grasped her hand and squeezed it. "We need time to address the matter."

Luke slapped the table. "Huh, I knew it. This holiday has taken us to places we least expected to go."

Sarah bit her lip, not knowing what to say.

Taylor squeezed her hand a second time. "Sarah's been the only sunshine in my life these past few days."

"I won't poke around too much," Taylor said, studying them intently. "It doesn't hurt to have a new friend, but I wish you didn't have to leave the resort."

Taylor shrugged. "I wish I could stay, but not having a job to compensate for the lodging adds expenses I least expected to pay."

"Will you be traveling home?" Luke asked, frowning.

"I can't infringe on Sarah's generosity forever. She's been terrific." Taylor's voice echoed with warmth, kindness while holding her hand. "You've probably already guessed it; I am planning to go home."

When Taylor looked at her, Sarah swallowed the disappointment, feeling her stomach twist into knots. It was too soon. She didn't want him to leave. Time, they needed time to get acquainted with each other, to learn whether a relationship could work.

"What do you think about Taylor leaving?" Luke asked. "The guy has to go home eventually. Where would that leave you?"

How should she respond to such brazenness? Sarah ignored Luke's question, shifting her focus to Taylor. His core essence called to her and whispered to her heart. They were in the early days of a relationship. What would happen if he left? The distance between them would be overwhelmingly great. His continent, her continent, and the Pacific Ocean, a massive body of water rolling between them. If he chose to leave, their relationship wouldn't stand a chance.

Her stomach twisted into knots.

She wasn't a selfish woman. She had to think of Taylor. The nurse inside her who always placed patient needs above her own, said, "Taylor must do what is best for him. That could be returning to Australia." Though she didn't want him to leave. Not now. Not ever. How would she cope if he left? Where would strength come from?

"My mother expressed similar concerns," Taylor said.

When he released his handhold, Sarah ached for his touch, grieving its absence like she'd mourn for him if he traveled to his home country. This cold separation hinted at mind-numbing loneliness. Though the decision should not be based on feminine whims, but rather on health and financial issues. She could only ensure this time on the mountain gave each of them joy.

Luke's face wrinkled as if trying to put the pieces of a puzzle together. He pointed at them. "There's something new here. I can sense it. In this, your mother might be wrong. Maybe you should stay, Taylor."

"Maybe," Taylor said, glancing at Sarah. "We'll figure it out."

Conversation droned on without her. Sarah strained to listen to the pair while pondering pine walls adorned with the odd elk head and customer notice boards. Luke ignored their relationship to talk about snowboarding. Was it difficult for Taylor to listen to cocky comments about jumps and edges when he couldn't do the same? Maybe the talk of winter sports wasn't appropriate, but that's what these two had in common. Whether the stories concerned Taylor or not, he didn't reveal emotion or prevent commentary that might disappoint Luke, but smiled and nodded often, drinking his beer, expressing kind generosity, and appreciating the return to the mountain.

He stared across the room where a collection of snowboards were stored in an outdoor rack, staring at them as if yearning to fly…and Sarah ached for him in that moment. She bit into a greasy fry, wondering why she'd ordered poutine. Taylor enjoyed a Mad Trappers burger and a beer. She watched his mouth as the beer glass touched his lips, repeatedly, drinking the beer as if it were water.

The server approached the table, wearing a bright red flannel shirt. He looked like a lumberjack. "Would you like another round?" the server asked.

"Yeah, mate," Luke replied, "I'll have a Coors Light."

Taylor stretched backward. "I'll have a Newcastle Brown."

When Sarah looked at him in a parental way, his brows rose in good humor. "No worries, Sarah," Taylor said, winking at her. "I'll only have two. This beer reminds me of my dad. It's one of his favorites."

Sarah shrugged. "I didn't say anything."

"You didn't have to. You're wearing your nurse face."

Luke seemed amused by the comment, laughter chortled from the base of his throat, but the niggling tone didn't upset Sarah. She laughed nervously, trying to appreciate the humorous situation.

"Okay, but you shouldn't drink alone," Sarah said, addressing the server. "I'll have the False Creek Raspberry Ale."

"The girl likes a fruity beer?" Luke asked.

"Love a fruity beer," Sarah replied.

When the drinks arrived, they cheered each other. Sarah thought she'd made a new friend. "To the mountains," Luke said.

Sarah clinked her glass against Luke's, then Taylor's, giving both men a meaningful stare. "To friends, and our time together."

It was time to shift his goals toward the future, though Taylor yearned for the past. As Sarah drove across a winter white parking lot, a wave of nostalgia settled in his thoughts. A yearning for days when health wasn't an issue.

The setting sun painted the mountain in a spectacular light show and as he took in that miraculous skyline: intense coral pinks, reds, and peachy orange, he remembered his journey. It wasn't that long ago he was laughing, celebrating, and storing his belongings in employee lodging. Now, they were collected and stored in the boot of the car, a suitcase, bedding, and the snowboard he'd brought with him from Australia. The board…its significance heightened his regret, calling to mind his love for the sport.

The stories Luke shared at lunch had hurt him, delivering regret and sadness no differently than a rip-curling wave, spawning a surge of jealousy and misery. Sarah broke into his depressed thoughts when she entered traffic on the motorway but turned left instead of right.

"Where are you going? This isn't the way to Calgary."

Sarah glanced at him serenely. "The conversation at the restaurant gave me the impression you're missing snowboarding."

"You noticed? Is it that obvious?"

"Given your brooding, it's pretty clear. Luke didn't notice your discomfort, but I did."

"Huh," Taylor said, staring straight ahead, "my friend takes pleasure in winter pursuits while I'm forced to recover. The accident and its circumstances are difficult to accept, but listening to Luke's exploits..."

"You mean, the bragging?"

"Well, Luke..."

Sarah nailed it. Luke was a good friend, but he had the tendency to focus on his own pleasures, his own needs. "He means well." *Why am I condoning the behavior?*

"He's insufferable," Sarah said, shaking her head. "I'm sorry you faced an injury, and what I'm about to say won't help, but you need to hear this. There's more to life than snowboarding, more to this province than mountains and snow."

Taylor frowned. "You sound like my mother."

Sarah gestured toward the mountains. "Taylor, look around you, there's an abundance of beauty here. Stellar mountains. One incredible sunset. I've seen many sunsets, but this one's spectacular."

"I'm not sure what you're suggesting, but I agree, it's beautiful. The sunset and the mountains." *Sarah*, she was spectacular, too.

"There's always remarkable sunsets in the winter. Wouldn't

happen without the wintry weather. I have a confession to make."

"What's that?" Taylor asked.

"I may live in a northern climate, but I've never enjoyed winter."

"That surprises me. How could anyone comment about a brilliant light show and not appreciate the season? You'd like it better if you took up winter sports."

"No way," Sarah said, stifling a laugh, "not on your life. It's too risky. I've seen *far* too many injuries, nursed one too many broken heads." *Hearts, too*. But Taylor kept this to himself.

"I get it, how caring for patients with serious injuries might frighten you from participating in winter activities, but I guarantee, you'd love it if you had the courage to try. I wish I could snowboard. I could get used to living here, despite the injury."

"I thought you might react that way." Sarah massaged the steering wheel. "There's a better view in Lake Louise. Would you like to see it?"

"The sun's setting. It'll be dark soon. Shouldn't we drive back?"

"What are you implying?" Sarah chuckled. "That a woman can't drive after the sun goes down? I've lived near the mountains my entire life. Driving at dusk doesn't concern me."

"How far is it to Lake Louise?"

"About thirty minutes."

Sarah spoke so quietly, Taylor wondered what she was thinking, or hiding? "What's up? Are you gaming me?"

"All right. I have kept a secret from you. How would you feel about a weekend getaway? You seemed disappointed while sharing a one-sided conversation with Luke."

Sarah sounded like an avenging angel. Taylor smiled. "I'd love to spend time in the mountains. It's what I came here to do."

"Good. I booked a room at the Post Hotel."

"You did? When did you do that?"

"When I escaped Luke's *blah blah blah* to visit the restroom."

Taylor laughed. The way Sarah delivered Luke's name amused him.

"We were fortunate. They had a room."

"You're a special woman, Sarah."

She glanced at him then, an appealing warmth in her eyes. In that moment, Taylor felt like the luckiest man alive. One minute sadness clouded his thinking, listening to his friend drone on and on…and the next moment he finds this gift.

Someone pinch me. Is this really happening?

"You're not too bad yourself," Sarah said.

Sarah looked directly at him and the warmth in her eyes, tenderness in her expression, caught Taylor off-guard. In the shadows of oncoming night, she shone like a twinkling star. The way her shoulder length brown hair dusted her shoulders, and the last vestiges of daylight sparkling in her eyes… She seemed happy. *Why?* Because they were traveling to Lake Louise? Or was it because she was in this car with him? He hoped her contentment arose because of him. Suddenly, he couldn't wait to reach the mountain hamlet.

THE WINTER LANDSCAPE shimmered with the final rays of sunlight as they drove toward Lake Louise. Though snow blanketed the edges of the motorway, the scenery caught Taylor's interest. Evergreens grew on either side of the road, their branches heavy with snow. Every now and then he'd glimpse mountains in the distance, and the scenery would paint a great picture with the subdued light.

My mother would love it.

At one point, a river the color of dark green emeralds flowed near the roadway, lined with snow on either side of its rocky banks. It sparkled in the waning light and Taylor thought the scenery was remarkable.

When Sarah pulled into the hotel's parking lot, the sun was setting behind the mountains. They climbed out of the car and Sarah opened her trunk. She reached for his suitcase.

"I'll get it," Taylor said, reaching for the case.

She patted his hand. "No, you won't. You're not supposed to lift heavy objects."

The case was heavy. "It weighs *more* than ten pounds," Taylor said, feeling incompetent. He understood his health limitations, yet guilt consumed him for not helping.

Sarah grasped the handle and struggled to slide the case over the lip. "What did you pack in here?" Her eyes sparkled with mischief. "A year's supply of clothing?"

"I planned on staying the entire season," Taylor said, deciding to take a risk. "Come on, let me help." Taylor grabbed the suitcase, and they lifted it over the edge together.

With the case sitting on frozen ground, Taylor noticed Sarah's gym bag.

"Do you have everything you need for this stay?" Taylor asked, gesturing toward the bag. "Cause I'm okay with lending a shirt or purchasing any essentials you might need."

"That's generous. I packed a few things, but if I need anything I'll buy it." Sarah grabbed the bag and slung it over her shoulder. She had this glint in her eyes that made him wonder: What was she thinking? What did she need? *Maybe me?*

"Were you planning this?"

Sarah's amusement glistened in her eyes like stars twinkling in the night sky. "Yes. Don't you like adventures?"

"I'm pleasantly surprised, that's all." Taylor stemmed deeper thoughts by studying the exterior of the hotel. The rustic building gave off a woodsy feeling. The nightfall and exterior lights highlighted the timber structure: logs lining its walls and the covered entranceway. The hotel suited the picturesque setting. He couldn't wait to get inside.

"I can manage the suitcase, if my nurse will let me."

Sarah closed the boot of the car then grasped the handle. "Not a chance. Nurse's orders."

Taylor smiled, but he raised his hands in exasperation. "Have it your way."

This woman had spunk. Sarah Evans might be slim in her physical build and diminutive height, but her voice intoned strength. Taylor appreciated her soldierly attitude, but his thoughts focused on feminine curves that a down-filled coat couldn't hide. She swayed while marching toward the hotel's entrance, pulling his suitcase over a rut-encrusted parking lot grooved with windrows of ice and snow.

Taylor admired Sarah, for her tenacity, her strength, even his care. He knew she meant well, but at times the nursing advice left him on edge. He should be taking care of her. He hid that thought.

"Do you see the skating rink?" Sarah asked, glancing at him.

An ice rink lay near the hotel's front entrance. Taylor had never seen an outdoor rink before. The surface glistened from strung fairy lights lining the circumference. The light drew him closer.

"That's cool," Taylor said. His excitement getting the better of him. Ignoring his injury, his age, he ran toward the rink and slid across the surface.

"No..." Sarah said, the warning coming too late.

She left their luggage in the middle of the parking lot and ran to his side in a flash, worry darkening her eyes. She grasped his waist. "Taylor, what are you doing? The surface is slippery...you could fall."

Balance did not concern Taylor. With Sarah standing so close, touching him, something in her eyes, in the way her lips parted, begged him to step closer. The icy surface was slippery. He wobbled...slid, but Sarah grasped his hands and helped him regain his balance. "Falling is the last thing on my mind."

"Taylor," Sarah said softy, squeezing his hand, "please, be careful."

"A woman's sympathy doesn't change my desires." Taylor looked at her meaningfully. "I want to take risks, to skate on this ice, to…" The passion swimming in Sarah's eyes, the way she stared at him…he wanted to make love to her. Was physical need off limits, too?

"To what? Tell me."

"I want time with you."

"Can I get your bags?" someone asked, calling from the doorway. Taylor disregarded the question. He wanted to kiss Sarah beneath the moonlight, and he suspected she might have the same desires.

"Yes, please," Taylor said, never losing the connection with Sarah.

The doorman gathered the suitcase and the bag from the parking lot, then placed their luggage on a trolley.

"Must we you go inside?" Taylor asked, grasping Sarah's arm.

"Maybe that's best? There's a chill in the air and it'll be cozier in *our* room." *Their room.* Taylor reflected on the cue. One word suggested this stay belonged to each of them, which encouraged movement toward that goal. They parted, but Sarah held fast to his hand, shuffling across the ice until they safely reached the hotel's front entranceway.

"Maybe I can skate, later?"

"Not on your life," Sarah said.

"You're a tough woman."

Inside the vestibule, the doorman handed Taylor a luggage tag. "Have a pleasant stay." He opened the main door.

"Thank you. We plan on it," Taylor said, eyeing Sarah, then together they entered the front hallway inside the lobby. The room exuded cozy comfort. Timber walls and red carpeting, comfortable seating set off to the right. An animal head on the wall compelled further investigation.

Taylor looked at Sarah, his eyes wide. "What is that?"

"A bison's head. Impressive, isn't it?"

"Definitely has a North American vibe."

They approached the front desk. Sarah said, "A room for Sarah Evans."

"It's my pleasure to assist you, Ms. Evans. Please, give me a minute," the clerk said, looking at her computer screen. "Ah…I have you and your partner booked for two nights."

"That's right."

"I have you in the Temple cabin. A lovely choice. Have you stayed with us before?"

"No," Taylor said. "We've been looking forward to it. We're excited to stay here."

"I'll need a credit card to guarantee the room."

Sarah reached into her purse for her wallet, but Taylor retrieved his from the inside pocket of his down-filled parka. "I've got this," Taylor said, passing the credit card to the clerk. Sarah gave him a surprised look, her hand on her wallet. "Please," he said quietly, whispering, "It's only right I pay the bill, especially after everything you've done for me."

Sarah nodded, leaving her wallet in her purse.

The clerk returned his credit card and handed him an information sheet. "We have two restaurants onsite. A fine dining restaurant and an 'English Style Pub' called *The Outpost*. There's availability at the spa if the two of you might be partial to a massage or a facial. Could I suggest a couples massage?"

Taylor glanced at Sarah and laughed inwardly, realizing

she was blushing. "Sounds perfect." Taylor liked the idea of a massage, other pursuits, too. "We'd enjoy that kind of relaxation. Wouldn't we, Sarah?"

Her lips rose into a grin. "Yes, sounds perfect."

The clerk passed Taylor a solid gold key and he accepted it.

"The doorman will bring your bags to the cabin. You'll find it through the doorway. Follow the pathway. The cabin is located on the third walkway to your right. I hope you enjoy your stay with us."

Taylor extended his hand and Sarah grasped his elbow. "Thank you. We plan on it."

CHAPTER ELEVEN

Sarah eyed Taylor as they left the main building, sensing his sorry attitude had improved. Sadness no longer shadowed his eyes and pouty lips were nowhere in sight. She was grateful for the adjustment and other feelings, too.

Taylor's jacket lay open to the waist. Sarah peeked at his belt line briefly, hoping he hadn't noticed the fleeting glance. The behavior, the sensual need, it embarrassed her, yet why should shame rear its ugly head? Women possessed feminine desires. What normal healthy female wouldn't reflect on a man's attributes.

Who are you trying to convince?

A gust of wind bristled against her skin, stealing her warmth, her breath. Snow swirled in the air. *Is Taylor cold?* If so, he didn't complain.

The wind blew again and experiencing its scale, Sarah shivered, wishing she had worn a scarf. Taylor must have noticed her discomfort as he reached for her hand. It felt right to slip her fingers into his handhold.

"Let's run," Taylor said. "There's more snow on this pathway than in my mother's freezer, and given the snowflakes swirling in the air, there's more snow to come."

"A bitter chill to go along with it."

Sarah squeezed his fingers and held on tightly as they raced across the frozen path. Banks of snow drifted on either side, swirling into the air. To their left, a few well-placed evergreens. Their boughs, heavy with snow, were lit with hundreds of tiny twinkling lights.

"Is Christmas coming?" Taylor said, laughing. "I can't believe how beautiful this is."

"It's magical," Sarah replied as they dashed past glistening white lights. "Though the frost in the air will freeze your face."

Taylor stopped at a secondary walkway. "It's romantic here, Sarah, and there's only you and I on the path."

"It's romantic inside the cabin, too, and warmer besides." Sarah urged Taylor to run with her along the path, leading them to their cabin.

"You ready for this?" Taylor asked, showing her the door key.

"I'm freezing, I need warmth," Sarah replied, stamping her feet on the doormat. "Open the door, let me in…"

Taylor placed the key in the doorknob and opened the door. He gestured for her to precede him inside. "After you, snuggle-pot."

Snuggle-pot? Feeling the chill in the air, Sarah passed through the doorway and into the cabin while considering the compliment. *Was that a compliment?* She faced Taylor as he closed the door. "What's a snuggle-pot?" Sarah asked, trying not laugh.

Taylor stole toward her, a huge smile on his face. "Aussie sweet talk. You'd have to read the work of author May Gibbs to get a better understanding of the term. I could also call you cuddle-pie if that suits you better."

"Hmm," Sarah said, snickering. "A difficult decision. Let me think about this, snuggle-pot."

Soft music singing from the TV drew Sarah's attention. That's when she saw the welcome message: "Good evening, Taylor, Sarah. Welcome to the Post Hotel." The missive imparted pleasant feelings.

"This is an amazing place," Taylor said. Suddenly he was behind her, wrapping his hands around her waist and pivoting her to face him.

"You sweet woman, I can't believe you did this for me, for us. I'm amazed. I'm grateful. Thank you so much."

"You're welcome."

"The cabin's spectacular."

It was no more than a small house, but the atmosphere gave numerous advantages. The rustic design: timber logs lining the walls, rustic paintings depicting local mountain scenery, and two love seats situated by a stone fireplace. Everything was perfect. Sarah couldn't wait to build a fire in the hearth. It all contributed to an inviting atmosphere. Maybe she was overthinking it, but the cabin also whispered romance. That couch by the fireplace, a cozy place for two to curl up while indulging in a glass of wine, a McIntosh Apple Riesling, or as in Taylor's preference, a cold one.

"I guess I made the right decision in booking the cabin. It's the perfect place for two to experience a weekend getaway."

"I agree." Taylor urged her closer and embraced her.

She clung to his arms. Being hugged like this comforted her. His breath dusted her forehead. His proximity enticed waves of nervous energy to muddle her brain, initiating naked desires to course through her veins, making it difficult to think let alone breathe.

Why the nerves? It was only a hug.

"You okay with this, Sarah? I mean, with the connection happening between us? If I'm not mistaken, it feels like we're progressing in this relationship." He studied her face as if her response was important. He touched her cheek, then stroked her skin gently.

Sarah took a deep breath. "Yes, I am. You've lived at my place for over a week. It's been great. We—you and I, this feels wonderful."

"Good. I hoped we were in agreement."

"Taylor, you're the perfect gentleman." It was true. He indulged her needs, behaving in a respectful way while contributing to her household. He wasn't rude or lazy, helped with the chores, whether that be tidying the kitchen or assisting with meals.

He smiled. "You have my father to thank for my shining example."

"Oh yeah, I'll thank him if we ever meet."

Sarah glanced across the room and saw the bed, one—queen-sized bed. One of them could sleep on the sofa, but did she have the nerve to lie beside Taylor? And what did that next step imply? They could experience intimacy on the mattress. Thinking about physical familiarities caused her temperature to rise. She swallowed the naked desires. Was that what she wanted? Intimacy? She supposed she had desired Taylor from the moment they'd met.

What did Taylor want?

Sarah shook off the insecurity, the worrying, wanting, waiting…

If the sleeping arrangement bothered Taylor, he didn't acknowledge it. "I love this cabin," he said, his happiness expressed through a ready smile. "You're amazing, Sarah. I'm so surprised. I can't believe you did this for me, especially at the last minute." Still wearing his down-filled jacket and winter boots, he released her, then walked across the room and lay on the bed. His head on the pillow, he crossed his hands behind his head. "I could get used to a place like this." He looked at her in a compelling way, his brows rising as a playful look blossomed on his face. And then a smirk. "Where are you sleeping? There's only one bed in this room unless there's a hidden bedroom in the closet."

His cheeky lopsided grin charmed her, disarmed her, too. "We're mature adults." She kicked off her boots and unzipped her coat. "If it's okay with you, I'll lay my head on the pillow next to yours. I prefer the left side of the bed."

"I don't mind sharing. Come on over." He shifted to the opposite edge then rolled onto his left side, patting her preferred spot. "Trust me, as you said, I'm the perfect gentleman."

Sarah didn't want Taylor to regard her with respect. She desired intimacy, affection, his strong arms wrapped around her, embracing her. *Telling me I'm his snuggle-pot.* His fingers massaging her skin and other sensitive spots; touching her, playing with her bra strap and the skin beneath the elastic. She studied his mouth, sighing, imagining tender kisses… several. And should romantic embers ignite into sensual flames, she might go all the way. She blushed, thinking about their bodies entwined, her cheeks heating.

"Penny for your thoughts?" Taylor asked. "You're quiet."

Sarah blushed. "It's nothing." She tried to downgrade their budding romance and turned away from his temptation while hanging her coat in the closet, then sat on the sofa. Self-conscious, she crossed her legs, shifting her foot up and down. What was the matter with her? She tapped her fingers on the armrest, trying to ignore the man on the bed, but her thoughts stimulated greater awareness simply from hearing him unzip his jacket.

"Sarah…"

She looked at Taylor. He seemed comfortable, sure of himself. He patted her preferred spot on the bed. "You're uncomfortable, and lonely, sitting on that loveseat all by yourself. Come over here. I've made a space for you."

Sarah studied Taylor's kind eyes and calm demeanor, desiring to lie beside him. But why not go to him, to explore the emotions firing between them? She wanted to get to know him better. God damn it, she wanted to slide her fingers underneath his T-shirt and touch his skin and taste his lips. They were in the perfect setting to make love, so why did doubtful thoughts intrude?

Was she right to want his friendship or had she made a mistake in booking this cabin? This romantic getaway? What did her actions suggest? Frack. She shook her head, dismissing the negativity: *'he'll only disappoint me like others before him'*, or the part of herself that ruminated about common sense and everyday values, or the negative Nelly who thought she wasn't good enough. For anyone.

Sarah reached for courage, rose from the sofa and walked toward the bed, then sat on the opposite side, offering Taylor her back. She was a mature woman. She wasn't a virgin.

Why am I playing shy?

"Is something wrong?" Taylor asked.

"I don't want to mislead you. Nor do I want to lead you on." She felt hopelessly lost, feeling like she wasn't good enough.

Taylor shifted closer. He touched her back gently, his fingers lingering on her spine before he rose upward to straddle the edge of the bed. He cupped her jaw. She looked at him, really looked at him. Curiosity radiated in his kind blue eyes while staring at her in an interested, heartwarming way. When he traced her jawline, tiny shivers traveled the length of her spine. She swallowed her nerves, sensing his need and recognizing her own.

"Sarah, there's no need to feel uncomfortable. No need to rush. You and I, we're two people on a journey. We don't have to pursue anything of an intimate nature unless the timing is right. We're newly acquainted, though regardless of what's happening here, you're a close friend. My friend."

That one comment helped Sarah relax. "We haven't known each other long, but it feels like we've always been close."

"This might sound crazy, but having spent time with you

this last week and a bit, our friendship reminds me of a long-lost friend."

When someone knocked on the door, Sarah was saved from replying. Taylor stretched away from her and sat a bit taller while Sarah responded to the interruption. The bellman brought their luggage inside, offered his pleasantries and then left. Sarah closed the draperies and returned to the bed. This time she reclined on the mattress, facing Taylor.

"Where were we?" Sarah asked.

Taylor smirked. "We were discussing friendship. When you lay your head on the pillow next to mine, you'll be safe. I'd never hurt you, never take advantage of you either. Never force you to act in a way that might make you uncomfortable. Unless…"

Sarah knew what 'unless' suggested, especially when he slid closer and massaged her cheek with his thumb, gently sliding the pad back and forth, causing warm shivers and goosebumps to rise on her skin. He stared at her in a sensual, needy way. It was difficult thinking let alone mind personal boundaries when he looked at her like that. Awareness tingled in her head, making it difficult to think let alone breathe.

"Unless what? What do you want?"

"To explore every inch of you."

Sarah swallowed. "Every inch? Taylor, I'm forty years old…"

"Almost an old maid." He smiled. "Five years older than me, imagine that."

"I haven't been with many men. I've never been married." She looked at him, exasperated, hopelessly lost, as if her lack of boyfriends summed up her lack of experience, making her less attractive and less desirous.

"What does age have to do with it? Age doesn't matter. And as for people you had sex with, well—I haven't had many relationships, if you know what I mean. But who cares about all that stuff, none of *that* matters. Furthermore, no other woman has cared for me like you, or nursed me to health like you. I'm in your debt."

"Is that the reason you like me? My nursing skills?"

"I respect you, regardless of your administrations."

Sarah fingered the duvet. "I'd provide care for anyone, even those less worthy. You're not beholden to me."

"There's more than 'care' happening here. I'm not sure how to describe it. The tension. The attraction?" As if to amplify the statement, Taylor brushed his hand against her arm. In response, her heart pulsed with longing, sexual longing. "And by the way, I'm no longer your patient, so we can leave the job responsibilities at the hospital where we first met."

Who was this bold-faced man lying beside her? She looked into his eyes, wondering. "You were easy to care for, easy to like." Easier still to fall for. Was she falling for Taylor?

"You'd be easy to love." He stretched forward and embraced her jaw, his free hand stroking her shoulder, warm breath fanning her face and smelling of mint. "What's happening between us, Sarah? I want to kiss you. May I kiss you?"

Sarah nodded, swallowing. "I thought you'd never ask. Yes, yes please…"

He urged her toward him. When their lips met, she closed

her eyes and moaned as if liquid candy was melting in her mouth, salivating as sweeter sensations surged through her. She breathed the scent of musk and spice while tasting mint. The kiss ended too soon.

"That was nice, Sarah."

She reached for Taylor and threaded her fingers through his hair. "Yes, it was. I need another kiss, and another after that, if you're willing."

"I aim to please, to satisfy your every desire."

"My every desire?" Sarah breathed deeply, shifting on the bed, leaning backward, and taking Taylor with her as she reclined to the pillow. He adjusted his position, his hand clutching her shoulder, his knee sliding between her legs, staring…the fire in his eyes attracted her like the pull of a magnet.

She was forty years old, too old to worry about repercussions. "I want kisses," Sarah admitted, looking at him hungrily.

He drew closer and leaned on one elbow. "Are we dating, then?" The question took her by surprise.

"I don't know. Maybe. In the heat of the moment, does it matter?"

"It does to me. Let's think this through," Taylor said, his fingers tracing a circular path on her belly. The change in sentiment was difficult to justify with his hand touching her. "Sarah, I don't sleep with a woman unless I'm in a committed relationship."

"Really?" Sarah asked, giggling nervously. "Not that I'm promiscuous, but who said we were dating? We were kissing. We were enjoying it. Taylor…I'm turned on enough to take it to the next level, and you're being, what…responsible? My desires are waning."

But one look at Taylor's face alerted Sarah to his seriousness. She watched his needy expression while contemplating his words. He rose upward, then reached for a strand of her hair and tucked it behind her ear.

"Maybe I'm being presumptuous, but my mother raised me to consider a woman's needs."

"Your mother's not here."

Taylor studied her meaningfully. "The lessons she instilled in me are. When I was a boy, we shared awkward conversations about sexuality." His brows rose, he laughed like someone embarrassed to make the confession. It endeared her to him.

"I bet you did," Sarah said, smothering her giggles while enjoying the amusement in his eyes.

Taylor fingered the sheets, massaging the fabric. "My father raised me as a gentleman." He looked at her. "To respect women. To put a ring on the finger if I found the right snuggle-pot." He studied her in a compelling way. "Both parents don't understand what's taking me so long."

"I don't think we're at that point." Sarah maneuvered closer to him and whispered against his mouth, "I hope your parents told you about personal protection, things like condoms, because I didn't bring any."

Taylor touched her lip, imparting a brief laugh. "Sarah, are you sweet-talking me? 'Cause your eyes are brighter than the sun," he said, licking her bottom lip. His tongue darting against her mouth almost undid her.

"Taylor, my desire increases with each passing minute."

"I'm on fire," Taylor said, his brows rising, "as hard as a rock, but once we cross this bridge..." he pulled her closer and she moved into his arms willingly. He grasped her neck, his fingers rising into her hairline. "...there's no turning back."

"I accept the consequences."

Taylor kissed her again. She wrapped her leg around his and slid her fingers beneath his jacket, then stole under his shirt and touched his skin. He jumped backward. "Sarah, your fingers, they're like ice."

Sarah laughed and helped Taylor remove his jacket. It landed on the floor. "Then warm them up."

CHAPTER TWELVE

Sarah's mood softened in the dining room, a place where pine walls oozed golden warmth and twinkling lights encircled the ceiling. The tables contributed to the romantic atmosphere, dressed in white linens, porcelain dinnerware and the smoldering radiance of a votive candle.

It was perfect. Taylor was perfect.

Euphoria washed over Sarah; long-lasting emotional excitement, harmonizing with physical sensations, stimulated by their lovemaking. No one had touched her like that before. Not rushed nor hasty, perhaps considering her needs. His sensitivity, his fingers wandering, taking her to passionate heights…pure bliss. She could still sense his hands, his fingers, flirting.

Sarah sipped a French Merlot, remembering, shivering. Practical by nature, she wasn't the type to rush into sexual encounters with men, but at forty years of age, she had no regrets.

"The way you touched me, kissed me, no one has loved

me like that before," Sarah said. "At least…" Was it crazy to share her feelings? She wouldn't usually take these kinds of risks.

"Go on," Taylor replied, "tell me."

"I've never felt like this before."

Taylor's lips lifted into a half-smile. He reached across the table and grasped her hand. His index finger massaged her forehand, tiny circles caressing her skin, helping her to relax. "Really? Never? That's a shame. You deserve hugs and kisses, especially with your commitment to patient care."

Sarah smiled slightly. "You're not obligated to hug or kiss me," Sarah said. "We didn't embrace because of my…" Nursing skills? She couldn't say it. She hoped he regarded the woman and not the professional nurse.

Taylor sipped his beer. "What were you about to say?"

Sarah sighed, admitting, "A consideration in regard to my nursing role."

"Hmm," Taylor said. "I respect you, but your professional career isn't what motivates me, just to be clear. I hugged you because passion fires between us, somewhere deep. It's been there from the start. You're a kind, caring person."

Sarah giggled. "You like my warm personality?"

"Yes, you're gorgeous, beautiful with your high cheekbones." Taylor placed his beer on the table. "But those eyes…"

"My eyes?"

"They glow warmer than the candlelight."

Sarah shook her head, emitting a soft sigh. "There must be more to it than drab hair and dull brown eyes."

"You'd never bore me," Taylor said, fingering the beer

glass. "My first memory of you, the moment when you held my hand, when you took my pulse, well, my heart did a flip-flop. I'm not imagining the emotion passing between us." Taylor took a deep breath. "I could hardly breathe. We made a connection."

Sarah giggled. "Your understanding of that moment had little to do with me. It was time for your pain meds."

"Sarah, *you* were my pain relief. My nurse, my long-lost friend. Meeting you…shifted my focus, turning pain into comfort," Taylor said, but then his expression soured into a frown. "I hate to admit this, but I'm a bit out of my element."

"Oh, how so?"

"Our relationship, this feeling, whatever it is, it's new to me. I came to Canada to snowboard but found an alluring woman instead. You tempt me, Sarah."

"I hope the change in plans doesn't disappoint." Sarah nibbled at her lip, worrying.

"The accident changed my perspective. I'm trying to come to terms with it. I'm glad we met, but I wish I'd accomplished what I set out to do."

"There'll be other opportunities."

"Not this year." Taylor grasped her hand again. He squeezed her fingers, staring at her in a reassuring way. "I'm overcome with emotion, from this amazing place, from the woman who's come into my life. Still, how did I find myself here? It feels like I stumbled into a bar, got drunk, and sobered to a new life."

Sarah thought about their introduction, that first day at the hospital when Taylor became her patient. She recalled that moment…the ruptured spleen; a severe injury, the sole reason

Taylor came into her care. "The journey hasn't played out the way you planned. I hope time in the mountains makes up for it. I hope my company and our friendship gives you joy."

He looked at her, his eyebrows rising. "You're not a replacement. I want to talk about what's happening between us."

"If not for the accident at the ski resort…" Sarah didn't want to say it. Didn't want to remind Taylor.

"We wouldn't be in this dining room," Taylor said. "Enjoying a meal by candlelight, sharing this view, sharing… well, I wouldn't be with you."

Sarah leaned backward in her chair and looked at Taylor. A brightness in his eyes had drawn her to him from the start. An explicable feeling: kindness, honesty, laid-back conversation. The first sign of humor caused his eyes to brighten. She liked it when he smiled. Her life was better, happier, richer because of him.

"Where do we go from here?" Sarah asked.

Taylor smirked. "The cabin comes to mind. I'd like to build a fire in the stone fireplace. So much to think about. So much to do."

Sarah grasped her wine glass. "A toast to a weekend in the mountains."

"Cheers," Taylor said, striking her glass. "To mountains, to moments like this, and the beautiful woman I have to thank for it all."

CHAPTER THIRTEEN

*L*ying in bed, Sarah stretched her arms above her head as sunlight streamed through a gap in the draperies. She lifted her hand, shielding her eyes from the light, recalling pleasant touches and sweet kisses. When she glanced to her right, searching for Taylor, he was no longer lying in the bed.

Where are you, Taylor?

She saw him sitting on the sofa; tousled hair and tired eyes, his thumb stuck in a magazine.

"Good morning. Did you sleep well?" Taylor asked, smiling.

"You're in a good mood," Sarah replied. "What time is it?"

Taylor glanced at his cell phone. "Just after eight. The change in time zone still has me waking up early."

"You must be hungry. You worked out last night."

They'd made love after dinner. Sarah smiled while recalling the intimacy: indulging in Taylor's embrace, his sweet kisses, the hand massage alone had sent shivers up her spine. After, her needs were fully satisfied. They were perfect together.

Could we be that couple? Maybe.

Taylor smirked, then rose from the sofa and walked toward her. Without hesitation, he crawled into bed and drew her into his embrace. Sarah lingered in the hug, beneath the sheets, not wanting the embrace to end. The caress warmed her. It felt natural. "I'm glad I booked this cabin."

"Me, too," Taylor said, kissing her. "What should we do today?"

"We should leave this bed," Sarah said, staring at his eyes. "I could stay here all day, but physical exercise this early in the morning won't agree with our plans."

"I wouldn't complain if our plans were to change."

Sarah sighed, stretching backward, his lips caressing her neck. "I'd mind…"

When Taylor kissed her, his lips massaging the sensitive tissues of her neck, his nearness tested her sensibilities, motivating her resolve to shift toward romance. A body and mind lacking in love tempted her to yield. She yearned for the affection that touched her waist, her skin, desiring to…engage in a third round of pleasure.

"The timing isn't right," Sarah said, struggling for control. "Maybe later…" Maybe he hadn't heard her appeal for he greedily caressed her neck, kissing her, heightening her need. She fought for control, considering this mountain gift, the one meant to inspire enjoyment of another kind. She grasped his cheek. Taylor's needs must come ahead of her own. "I want to show you the hamlet: the lake, the chateau…we could go for a gondola ride."

Taylor lay beside her, staring, the wonder in his eyes greeting her with desire. "Sounds great. I'm *up* for anything."

Sarah swallowed. "There's a restaurant at the top of the mountain. It has an amazing view."

He smiled. "I appreciate a good view. I have one right here." He stared at her strangely. What did the behavior insinuate? Was he hungry, and if so, for what?

"Why are you looking at me like that? What are you thinking?"

"Me?" Taylor replied, pointing at himself. "Nothing devious, I'm happy sharing this space with you. I don't care what we do as long as we do it together. Though I hate to admit it…I'm hungry."

Sarah giggled. "I can tell. Your stomach's rumbling." She nuzzled closer, startling Taylor when she patted his belly. "I'm still salivating from last night's delicacy and I'm not talking about the crème brûlée." Sarah giggled. "Though a cup of coffee would be a good start to the day."

Taylor touched her nose. "Why don't we get out of bed and have a shower."

"Alone, or together?"

Taylor threw off the sheets, reached for her and pulled her into his embrace. "Together. This adventure starts now." Sarah squealed with laughter as she left the bed in Taylor's arms.

"Taylor," Sarah said, protesting, squirming, "you're not supposed to lift anything heavy, and that includes me."

He laughed as he carried her through the doorway and

into the bathroom. She didn't miss the twinge at the corner of his eye. "You're not heavy. You're slight, small."

"That's what you said before…"

When Taylor frowned, Sarah worried about his still healing spleen. He didn't let her fall while assisting her to her feet. "Are you okay?"

He shrugged, rubbing his side. "I'm fine. I'll be fine."

If the injury worried Taylor, he didn't complain while reaching inside the shower to turn on the water. When the water streamed from the spout at a cozy temperature, he removed his pajamas, all the while studying her in an appreciative manner, then walked inside the stall. Sarah stood outside the stall, watching streaming water and the man; a fully masculine physique, strong arms, slim chest, his... *Oh my.* Sarah swallowed, sigh...

"The water's warm," Taylor said.

"If Michelangelo could sculpt you, you'd never leave this shower. You're a masterpiece, a work of art."

"What?" Taylor burst into laughter. "No one would dare sculpt me let alone paint my portrait, well…maybe if I was holding a beauty like you. Are you coming in?" Taylor asked, smirking. He held a bar of soap and massaged it against his chest in circular motions, creating a thick lather that bubbled and flowed along his flat stomach and his legs to the shower floor.

Sarah swallowed her apprehension, removed her pajamas and tossed them on the floor as if they were insignificant, then walked into the stall. Taylor pulled her close and closed the door. He gently ushered her into the spray where warm water streamed against her skin, their skin. Sarah laid her hand against his chest, the spot where he'd been hurt. The bruising lingered, yellowish brown and green, the colors were diminishing, and all the while delicious heat, water and need, steamed between them.

"Can I wash your back?" Taylor asked.

"Yes, please."

CHAPTER FOURTEEN

Taylor stood near Lake Louise's shoreline, appreciating the view: a frozen lake rimmed with white, evergreens blanketed with snow, and majestic mountains towering in the distance, higher than one's imagination could climb. It was different observing the scenery without a snowboard in his hand, but the change didn't trouble him.

Sarah pointed at the distant mountain. "That's the Victoria Glacier."

"I can't get over the color of the lake. Clear, aquamarine ice, the surface larger than the space at the hotel," Taylor said. "It's magical."

"I agree, it's pretty incredible."

Taylor stepped closer. "The ice mirrors the mountain, magnifying the wonder. I wish I could strap on some skates and join the adventurers."

Bundled in winter gear, people were skating. Some held hands while other visitors walked around the lake's circumference on a gray pathway frosted with white. Taylor wanted to get closer still, so he left the pathway and stepped onto the rocks. "Absolutely incredible."

"Yes, but I wish the weather was warmer," Sarah said.

As if in response to her words, the wind gusted, sending a blast of icy air against his open neckline. The draught prickled his skin, causing an instant need to escape the chill and return to summer weather. *Summer had arrived in Australia...* He shook off the discomfort and zipped his jacket, pulling the woolen cap over his ears.

Taylor glanced at Sarah. "The scenery takes my breath away. Literally—it's unbelievably cold."

Sarah nodded, visibly shaking.

Taylor knew Sarah brought him to Lake Louise to add joy to his life, to chase away regrets, and though his skin was freezing, happiness bubbled inside. "Thank you for this. What an incredible place."

Sarah marched in place. "It's special all right. I love coming here. There's only one downside. This!" She pointed nowhere in particular. "This incredibly bitter weather."

"Given the view, I'm not sure that's a disadvantage."

"You say that like a hardened Canadian." Sarah imparted a brief laugh, her breath steaming from her lips, yet smiling through the displeasure. She was either fearless or bore the cold for him. "This time of year, the scenery comes with frigid temperatures. Lake Louise is only forty-five minutes from Banff, but I always find it cooler near the lake. I prefer visiting the area in the summertime."

If Sarah accompanied him, he'd enjoy this view any time of year. "If not for the injury, I'd probably see it differently."

"I'm sure you would. There's a ski hill at Lake Louise. This is strictly my opinion, but Lake Louise is renowned for its beginner runs."

"Who said I was a beginner?" Taylor asked, laughing. "I can't imagine seeing this wonder at any other time of year. It wouldn't be the same without the snow." Taylor returned his focus to the glacier. "I read the pamphlet at the hotel. We could hike around the lake, take a sleigh ride, maybe grab a drink at the Château."

Sarah stared at him in a prickly way. "Hike? In this weather? Are you kidding me?"

"Do you want to leave? Go someplace warmer than a frozen lake?" Everything in her demeanor, her awkward posture, her scrunched-up face, screamed raw discomfort.

"How about an exciting alternative. There's an ice bar," Sarah said. "A hot drink might lessen the chill." She danced toward the pathway.

Taylor followed her. "An ice bar? Really? That's amazing. I have to experience that. What are we waiting for? Let's go."

They hiked along the pathway lining the perimeter of the lake. Sarah walked slightly ahead of him, maintaining a good pace, but still noticeably cold. He wanted to shield her from the discomfort. Maybe he could help. "Can I hold your hand, Sarah?"

She slowed the pace while showing off her hands, revealing bright orange mitts. A playful look brightened her expression. For him? Nah…she probably longed for warmth more so than a hot drink, but he hoped Sarah enjoyed his company.

She grasped his hand. "Yes, you may. I'd like to hold your hand."

Taylor squeezed her mitten-covered hand; holding her made him happy. He forgot the chill in the air while urging her closer. And that distant torment in her eyes, *(from the cold?)*, warmed into a radiant smile.

"You must see the Château. The ice bar is near the entrance."

Sarah's lips pursed. She frowned, shrugged. Clearly, Sarah wanted more than a mountainous view and frigid temperatures. Did she want him? "Let's go to the hotel," Taylor said. It was the only way to end the discomfort.

Sarah didn't argue. "The entrance is near the ice bar. You must see it."

IN THE END, Taylor's excitement was contagious. Sarah endured the elements a bit longer while enjoying a drink at the ice bar. The sacrifice was worth it. Taylor's excitement was contagious. The arctic chill didn't seem to affect him, his face shone with intrigue, his cheeks pink and eyes bright, simply from admiring ice blocks walling the bar. And though the bar was an incredible feat of art, she'd never seen anyone draw their fingers across ice that way before, like he appreciated the artist's effort. How would he react when she showed him the ice castle?

Sitting near the fire pit, Sarah sipped the cocktail warmer *Glacier Express*, hot mint tea infused with maple rye and bitters. Smooth and hot, the alcohol added a minty kick, warming her from the inside.

Taylor sipped hot apple cider. "*Flake it 'til you make it*?" Taylor said, laughing. "Who named this cocktail? Though the maple and rye combo taste good together. Try it."

Before Sarah could say yes please or no thank you, Taylor passed the drink to her and she passed hers to him. Though she savored the hot apple flavor, her focus remained on Taylor. He watched her intently.

What's the matter with him? The cold doesn't affect him. If anything, he appreciated the mountain adventure and viewed it in a unique way. Who represented the real Canadian here?

"It's delicious. I wouldn't mind one more. Should we request a second round?" Sarah asked.

Taylor returned her drink. "I don't think so. You're shivering."

"I'm okay," Sarah said, returning his drink. She didn't want to complain, didn't want to ruin Taylor's return to the mountain.

"You're a generous host." He sipped his drink. "The bartender told me there's shops inside the hotel. He says they have the perfect gifts for couples, especially couples in love." Taylor smiled, giving her a wink. "Chocolate, Canadian souvenirs, jewelry and other things. Says he knows love when he sees it."

"Oh yeah?" Sarah giggled. "How did you respond? Did the word 'love' scare you away?"

Taylor leaned toward her. "Words don't frighten me. I didn't deny it, either."

"You didn't?"

"Nope." Taylor shook his head, studying her in a heady way.

Sarah stared at him, open-mouthed, her heart in her hands. After a few seconds, she sipped her tea. Whatever Taylor was feeling, thinking, he didn't acknowledge it. To her, their patient/nurse relationship had blossomed into a strong friendship, seemingly overnight. She had a vague awareness of 'extreme likability' and that courtesy was good enough for now.

"I'm partial to you as well," Sarah said, glancing away. *I love your Australian accent.*

He grasped her hand. "You're beautiful with your cheeks blossoming like an Alberta rose. It's from this beastly snow. You probably want to escape the weather, to go where it's warmer."

To receive a lover's gift? "Possibly."

"Me?" Taylor pointed at himself. "I want a kiss."

Sarah giggled. "Right here? Now?" What did she want? She'd suffer the weather, hot or cold, for a heartwarming kiss. She didn't care who was watching, either. "Why don't you?" She teased.

He bent toward her and pressed his advantage, kissing her. Ice-cold lips settled against her mouth and the sensation stimulated awareness, caressing her need. The meeting of cold and warm teased her senses, leaving her greedy for another kiss. She returned Taylor's affection and kissed him, too.

He breathed deeply, his face close, studying her in a potent way. It was difficult to retreat from his hug, to let space and winter come between them again. "Let's go inside, Sarah."

She nodded. "Do you want a second drink?"

"I'm sure there's drinks inside the hotel. Let's go, save you from this wintry weather."

SARAH LOOKED beyond the picture glass windows at the Fairview Restaurant, admiring the Victoria Glacier in the distance. "This is how I appreciate life. Here, in the warmth of a dining room, I'm not burdened by the sometimes unpleasant nature of winter. I mean, don't misunderstand me, winter has its charm, its likability, but this restaurant and its picture-perfect view is the best place to contemplate life."

Taylor sipped his tea, studying her in an earnest way. "I'm an easygoing guy. I don't mind admiring the view, who doesn't appreciate a good view, but if my health were better, I'd be one with the elements: snowboarding."

"Not me."

"Why? Because the temperature makes you uncomfortable?"

"In part."

"You can overcome the chill by layering. Dress for the weather; undershirts, sweaters, vests and other winter gear."

Sarah sipped her tea. "Or…enjoy the view."

"Don't get me wrong," Taylor said, leaning backward and crossing his arms, "Afternoon Tea is great, dainty sandwiches and pastry squares. My father has an English heritage, so scones with clotted cream remain my favorite part of the custom."

Sarah grasped a sandwich wedge filled with thinly sliced cucumber and cream cheese. "For me, it's the entire experience. Afternoon Tea should be seasoned with good company and time, tasted, and not rushed."

"Aha…so that's what we have in common, you and I, we enjoy experiencing life. That's why I snowboard. It's why you dine, admiring the view. It's the same concept."

"Not exactly," Sarah said. "You can't compare sports to dining."

"Why not?" Taylor asked. "Living life is living life, though everyone has different expectations."

"One breaks a leg or ruptures a spleen while the other adds thought and consequence."

Taylor drummed his fingers on the table. "I won't take offense to the injury comment," he said, frowning, "but what is the consequence of Afternoon Tea?"

Sarah nibbled at her lip before grasping a scone and heaping it with a healthy dollop of Devonshire cream. "Tantalizing your taste buds and probable weight gain."

"Hmm." Taylor laughed, shaking his head. "I've never worried about food. The exercise takes care of the caloric intake." He grasped a scone and applied the same fixings, though he added a spoonful of strawberry jelly to the clotted cream. Sarah watched as he indulged, biting into the rich confection. A spot of red coated the corner of his lips. Sarah stared at that spot, at his strawberry lips, thinking she'd like to rise from her chair, circle the table, and lick at the jelly. That would show this man her adventurous nature.

"Why are you looking at me like that, with those gorgeous brown eyes of yours?" Taylor asked.

Sarah blushed. "I'm reflecting on a part of the experience that's never occurred to me before."

"Sarah, you're smiling."

She stretched forward. "You have a spot of jelly on the corner of your mouth."

He reached for the napkin to clean his face, but Sarah grasped his hand and held it tightly. "Would it be rude to lick the strawberry jelly off your face?"

Taylor looked around, and though the comment seemed to surprise him, his lips rose into a grin. "There are other people in the dining room, but you said we should experience life. I challenge you to go for the lips, I won't stop you." He had the audacity to wink.

When Sarah stood, Taylor slid his chair back. She minded the gap without hesitating and sat on his lap. Taylor's eyebrows lifted in surprise, and she perused the charismatic color in his blue eyes, a marvel intriguing her in ways the mountain view beyond the picture window could never bestow.

"You have me in a heightened state," Taylor said. "What are you waiting for?"

Sarah licked at the strawberry jelly from the corner of his lips. She closed her eyes as Taylor embraced her and kissed her. That kiss lingered, lasting an indeterminable time. When they finally drew apart, a couple near to them clapped their hands. Embarrassed by the attention, Sarah lowered her head and returned to her chair.

Taylor edged his chair closer to the table. "My oh my, I see what you mean about consequence. The kiss fueled an inner desire I've never known before. The best experience I've had while experiencing Afternoon Tea." Taylor touched his mouth.

"Better than snowboarding?" Sarah asked, her only desire to kiss Taylor again.

"As you say, you can't compare the two events, though Afternoon Tea has an entirely new meaning."

"Only while dispensing the consequence of jelly."

"A thoughtful experience, for sure."

Their circumstances presented pleasurable options. They were compatible, but the closer they became the more Sarah worried. They hadn't discussed one important matter yet. If their relationship continued, where would they live?

CHAPTER FIFTEEN

This place embraced potential. Sarah lay on the bed embraced in the warmth of Taylor's arms, her head against his chest, his fingers brushing her hair, massaging her scalp, currying the sweetest of sensations. Sarah listened to his heartbeat, steady and strong. The thrum of it comforting, a stronger sensation than the odd spark discharging from the fire in the hearth.

Taylor's touch fulfilled a need, satisfying the affection missing from her life—*love*.

She desired love.

If anything were to spoil this tenderness, this friendship, her heart would break. Her spirit had broken before and it could happen again. When the heat of new love diminished like the last embers of a fire, relationship flaws always rose to the surface, in most men she'd dated. Problems intruded, spoiling everything. It must be her shortcoming, her failure or weakness, or some character trait previous partners hadn't appreciated.

Would Taylor be different?

Sarah reached for the mountain duvet cover and tugged it upward covering her hips. "What's happening between us?" she asked. "Is this for real?"

Taylor wound a strand of her hair around his finger. "We've made love twice in one day. It feels…"

"…blissful," Sarah said. But regardless of their romantic connection, doubt stole into her thoughts. "Our romance feels too good to be true." She rose upward, leaned on one elbow, and stared at Taylor's electric blue eyes. "Where do we go from here? I mean, the foreplay rocked my world, the orgasm a ten out of ten, but when the physical attraction wears off, what comes next?"

"Does it matter? Can we enjoy the here and now without worrying about the after-effect?" Taylor looked at her seriously. "But humor me. What do you want? Tell me."

"An assurance our relationship means more than sex."

Taylor smiled wryly. "I don't mean to diminish your concern, but…the sex, mind-bending."

Taylor stated the facts like she'd given him the best gift in the world. If mussed hair, a sexy afterglow, and pleasurable emotions supported this theory, he meant every word. They shared a strong connection, but the physical aspects were not relevant to this discussion.

"Sure," Sarah said, blushing, "but the moment we became intimate, I was in deep." She always gave with her heart. Maybe her sensitivity shaped the issue.

"If I'm honest about my feelings, I found myself attracted to you from the moment you held my wrist and took my pulse." Taylor grasped her hand. "These fingers," he said, stroking, "the things they did to me, do to me."

Sarah smiled, expelling a nervous giggle, then lay against his chest once again. "I have a strong grip. As I recall, your heart pumped a little too fast. You were in pain. Maybe I'm overreacting. Maybe fear shouldn't intrude in our relationship."

"Would it help to name the affliction? What's worrying you?"

Sarah sighed. "Honestly, it's what comes next: your country or my country. If our relationship continues, where do we live?"

"That's a tough question. I'm not sure how to respond to that right now." He released her hand and stretched backward, putting his head on the pillow. "We've been intimate, but we haven't made a commitment to each other. If this *bliss* continues, if we want it to continue, would you relocate to Australia?"

It's so far from home.

"Hmm," Sarah said, considering the idea. "Moving raises more questions than answers. I'd have to sell my place, pack my bags, and get on a plane…"

"You wouldn't have to sell straightaway. You could rent your place. I could help with rental prospects given my mortgage career."

"I'd be leaving a lot behind." *My friends, My family…* "I can't pack everything that matters in a suitcase."

"I get it. There's a lot to consider. I'm only asking because after losing my job at the ski resort, I have no income to support a lengthy stay in Canada."

Focused on her own circumstances, Sarah said, "I'm not sure I could do it."

"I understand," Taylor replied. "My parents are in their senior years. We're close. I call my mom most days."

"Every day?" Sarah glanced at Taylor.

"I know it gives the impression of neediness, but calling my mom makes her happy."

Sarah nodded. "That's kind of you. Would you do the same for me?"

Taylor touched her nose. "Twice a day for you."

Sarah's lips lifted into a wry half-smile. "If you're not in the country, I'll accept the charges."

Taylor sighed. "I had no idea I'd meet someone special, but it's happened. Is this the right time to consider a change? We're still in the discovery phase, but if our relationship continues, one of us has to relocate." He hesitated, breathing deeply. "Moving, for either one of us, is a sacrifice. A lot to consider."

"Leave Canada…" For a man she'd just met. That thought struck home. Sarah had never contemplated such a life-altering decision, though she'd never expected to care for a man from another country either. The newness of the relationship didn't matter. She was attracted to Taylor, but before her heart dug in completely, she needed to think this through.

"I don't know," Sarah finally said, searching his eyes for an answer that couldn't be found. "It's a lot to consider. Maybe if we'd dated longer I'd have a better response."

"I have to go home," Taylor said, his tone worrisome, "at some point."

Sarah nodded. "You state your case as if you've already booked the flight." The finality of an airline ticket troubled Sarah. Her gut twisted; her heart ached. Their relationship might be new, yet she couldn't stand the thought of separation. Hopefully, they'd resolve the issue in an amicable way.

"What about you? You're here, you could stay. Would you, for me? I'm a nurse. If health complications arose, if your pain increased, I could help."

Taylor smiled. "You're an incredible nurse, a sweet woman, but it wouldn't be right to burden you." He pulled her into his arms and kissed her forehead. "I want you; I want to reach deeper places in your life, but let's not trouble ourselves. Leave today's worries and tomorrow's plans for another day."

"We have to talk about it."

"Of course, we do. I understand, but let's put this conversation aside for now. I have something special in mind."

"What's that?" Sarah asked, not wanting to talk about it either.

"A bath. You game?"

"In the whirlpool tub? Yes," Sarah said.

Taylor climbed out of bed and stood there, looking like an Adonis. He stared at her with his perfect pecs, scratching his side, frowning slightly. "I'm good at preparing a bath. Too bad we don't have bath salts."

Sarah watched Taylor approach the foot of the bed, muscular arms, nice chest, and jockey shorts shielding his God-given gifts from her view. He strutted before her, walking to the bathroom, radiating enthusiasm and interests she could only guess at. Was he keeping something from her? It wasn't long before she heard running water.

Taylor returned. "Come on, let's go, the water's waiting." Taylor threw off the sheets and grasped her hand. He led her to the tub.

Sarah giggled, standing near the tub in scanty clothing, a lacy tangerine bra and matching panties. "How's the water? Did you test it? I'm not entering the bathwater unless it's the perfect temperature."

Taylor tested the temperature. "Trust me, it's perfect." He gestured toward the tub. "After you, sweetheart."

Sweetheart? Sarah liked the endearment and appreciated what the term implied. With only a moment's hesitation, she removed her bra and panties and tossed them on the floor. She felt awkward standing near Taylor, completely naked, but the way he studied her, perusing her as if he adored her nakedness, inspired confidence.

"Sweet heaven," he said, extending his hand, "let me help you."

Eyeing him, Sarah grasped his fingers. "What is it?"

"You're stunning," Taylor said. "It's not only your silky skin or your…"

Sarah laughed. "My boobs?"

"Well, they're amazing. I can't stop looking at them, or touching…"

"Compliment accepted." Sarah stepped into the tub, feeling good about herself, feeling better about this relationship. The water held the perfect temperature, and the heat only amplified their steamy connection. "I'm the lucky one," Sarah said. She was lucky, but only if this relationship succeeded.

Taylor removed his jockey shorts and joined her in the tub. They lounged in the water, facing each other, their legs overlapping. "I could stay this way forever." Sarah stretched forward and grasped his upper thigh.

Taylor's eyes rose when her fingers strayed too close to his private parts. "Whoa, woman. Here? In the tub?"

"No silly," Sarah said. "You and me, like this, together forever."

Taylor frowned. "It's a great tub but it's a bit small. You enjoy it. May I wash your back?"

His hands were swirling in the water, he looked everywhere but at her. She moved her hand away from his leg. "What's wrong?"

Taylor rose from the tub, grabbed a towel and wrapped it around his waist. "There's not enough room in here for two." He reached for a bar of soap, unwrapped it, then knelt beside the tub.

"You can tell me," Sarah said, feeling his hand on her back. "Is it your spleen?"

Though Taylor washed her skin, the circular motions only heightened the anxiety that foamed between them. "It's not my health, though my side is always tender. But that's not what's hurting right now."

He shrugged, looking at her as if he had suffered a new injury. "Sarah, I booked my flight home a week ago."

The news chilled her like a shot of ice water splashing against her face. What should she say? How should she respond? How could she cope with the shock, the disappointment? In a tub of warm water, she shivered, feeling awkward and much too naked. She cupped her breasts, trying to hide them from his view, then stood, the water sluicing down her body.

"Sarah…"

She studied his face, bearing the regret in his eyes. She understood discontent; she'd witnessed injuries, pain, many times before. But this time, this potential ending induced the worst heartache. Anguish raced through her heart.

"You booked a flight without telling me? Why?"

Taylor grasped a towel and passed it to her. "I'm telling you now, I don't know."

"What don't you know?" Sarah wrapped the towel around herself, concealing herself from his view, anger and disappointment permeating every pore. Every man she'd ever known had hurt her. Why should this one be different?

Taylor appealed to her with upraised hands. "I didn't grasp the situation; about you, about us. I booked the flight before the cabin, before we made love, before you made me *feel* loved." He paused. "Sweetheart, you've captured my attention. My imagination…"

"Don't call me sweetheart," Sarah said bleakly. "Not because I don't desire the endearment. It's just, it hurts too much."

He continued as if he hadn't heard. "Let me explain." He appealed with both hands. "I'm worried about my finances, my health, and the injury. The left side of my abdomen is always in pain." He massaged his hands through his hair. "There's medical insurance to consider as well. I booked the flight. I made a difficult decision, and it feels wrong."

Sarah slumped into the tub. The water sloshed, spilling over the lip and onto the floor. The towel slipped beneath the water. The fabric edges absorbed the liquid. She shook her head, wrapping the towel firmly around herself, hiding herself, shielding her vulnerability from his perusal as if she needed to protect herself from her own pain.

How would she cope? Taylor leaving hurt her in places she hadn't perceived before. Past boyfriends and their various issues made Taylor's imminent departure too easy to accept.

"When do you leave?" Sarah asked.

Taylor sank to the floor. He reached into the water and grasped her hand. "Friday night," he said with a grimace, his tone sorrowful and quiet.

Sarah nodded.

"I should have prepared this bath better." Taylor lifted her upward, embracing her, wet towel and all. "I'm sorry." He embraced her face and stroked her cheek with his thumb. "The water's not nearly warm enough."

Sarah glanced at Taylor momentarily, tears building in her eyes, standing like a statue in his arms. "I'm cold."

"Hey, traveling home doesn't mean it's over. Doesn't mean *we're* done."

The concept of home held less appeal without Taylor's friendship. No social conversation, warmth, or comfort. His leaving implied a return to loneliness without someone to share life's experiences. Didn't he understand that? He'd already said the distance could be a problem. But Taylor was right. An airline ticket didn't equal an end to their relationship. Flights could be rebooked, her need to stay in Canada could alter as well.

Sarah did the math. "We have five days." Five days would go by fast. Thinking about their limited time, Sarah became emotional. She looked at Taylor with tears in her eyes. He seemed like he might cry, too.

"Sweetheart," Taylor said. "Let's make the most of our time together."

CHAPTER SIXTEEN

Taylor sat on the sofa, facing the decision that could affect the rest of his life. Sarah's reaction to the flight plan had left him reeling. Her surprise, her hurt, alerted him to her true feelings. She hadn't expressed relationship goals, her inner desire or hope for the future prior to that moment, yet grief expressed through tears revealed her position.

Sarah didn't want him to go.

How can I leave?

Taylor had strong feelings for Sarah. *Do I love her? Is that why this guttural ache hurts so much?* It was horrible instigating sorrow when Sarah had given him gifts other woman had never imparted.

What should I do?

Booking the flight had seemed necessary, given his medical needs and financial situation, but now…he wasn't sure he'd made the right decision.

He heard Sarah's muffled voice, speaking to someone on

her cell phone in the bathroom. Her mother? A friend? Getting advice? The conversation elevated his guilt. He'd shown a lack of judgment and felt like a heel.

Taylor was still sitting on the sofa when Sarah opened the bathroom door and strode into the room. Wrapped in a soft white bathrobe, she was wearing matching hotel slippers. His need flared to life. Sarah stood at the threshold, quietly staring, expressing vulnerability. She touched her lips, her flushed face, breathing heavier. Worry underscored her eyes.

Taylor swallowed at the sight of one incredible woman. How could he leave her? Given how his heart ached, this might be love.

Sarah sighed. "I spoke to my supervisor at work. I'm taking a leave of absence."

His eyes went wide. "Really? That surprises me. Why?"

Sarah walked across the space and sat near him on the opposite sofa. When she leaned forward, he was given an enticing view of her cleavage, which made it difficult to think. She must have noticed where his vision strayed as her lips lifted into a sultry half-smile. "Taylor, if we only have five days together, I want to share every minute with you. How do you feel about that?"

Taylor smiled. "How do I feel? I'm grateful you're with me."

"If it's okay, we could stay in the mountains. In this cabin if the hotel will extend the reservation."

"Sounds like a plan. I'll call the front desk and check if the room's available beyond the weekend," Taylor said. "There's only one problem."

"What's that?"

Taylor pointed at the bed. "There's only one bed. Will you share it with me?"

Sarah nodded. She reached for his hand. "Yes, I will."

"Even though I'm leaving?"

"I'm aware," Sarah said, sighing. "I'm not happy about it."

Taylor grasped her hand and squeezed. "I'm not excited about it either. Leaving you isn't easy. I'm not sure what traveling home means for us in the long term, but I don't want to lead you on, nor do I want to hurt you," Taylor said. "I have to go."

Sarah looked at the floor. "I understand."

Taylor tipped her face upward and stared at her sorrowful eyes. "Do you?"

Sarah nodded. "I'm worried."

"What worries you most?" That he'd never kiss her again.

"The first promising relationship will end because of the distance."

"You don't know that," Taylor said, shifting to the other sofa. When he looked at her eyes, he realized Sarah was on the verge of tears. "If we're meant to be together, we will be together."

Sarah nodded. "You make it sound simple." Those brown eyes: a pool of sorrow, threatening to spill.

"Sarah, don't cry." Taylor brushed brown strands highlighted with blond away from her eyes. "I would never hurt you."

"Maybe," she said, her voice wobbling. "Not intentionally. You're a kind man."

Taylor pulled Sarah into his arms, and she lay against him, her head against his chest. When Friday arrived, what would he do? He supposed it was wiser not to think about that day right now. Better to do everything in his power to make the next five days as special as they could be.

"Should we plan for the week ahead?"

Sarah wiped her eyes. "Definitely."

CHAPTER SEVENTEEN

Sleep hadn't come easy. Sarah had lain awake most of the night consumed with anxiety and thoughts that wouldn't quit, worrying about Taylor and the flight to Sydney. *Australia? It was so far away.* Why had she chosen to date a foreigner? Of all the relationships she could have pursued, this one came with the most risk.

Sitting at the breakfast table, Taylor looked at her in a hungry-like-the-wolf manner, perhaps crossing the lines of propriety, caressing her sensitivity, with care, need, and humor. No man's touch rivaled his. When he left, his absence would carve a hole in her heart.

She'd miss him.

Sarah sipped her morning coffee, frowning.

"What should we do today?" Taylor asked, slicing into an applewood sausage.

He smiled as if they had nothing to worry about, a cheeky lopsided grin suggesting an idea was taking shape. She pondered his upturned lips, his inner light, and the apparent happy mood eased her apprehension. "That's easy, you and I, together."

He winked, chewing. "I have an idea."

"What's that?"

"I want to experience as much as I can in these last days. Let's skate, at the hotel or Lake Louise."

Sarah's face paled. "You —Skating— Uh-uh. No way." She shook her head. "It's not happening. Your spleen's not fully recovered. If you fall…"

"*If* I fall," Taylor said, laughing under his breath. "Relax. If we're together twenty-five years from now, will you care for me like you do now?"

Sarah's eyebrows rose. "Do you think there's a chance?"

"Why should it surprise you?" Taylor reached across the table and grasped her hand. "Nothing's impossible if we both want it. It won't be easy. Not at first. I might experience another accident."

"I don't doubt it," Sarah said, unamused. "Reason enough for you not to skate. Do you have experience? Have you skated before? One slip, one fall, could send you back to the emergency room."

"You'd like that. An accident would prevent me from boarding Friday's flight," Taylor said. "A mishap is as unlikely as occupying another hospital bed."

Sarah frowned.

"You're wearing your nurse face again," Taylor said, slightly amused.

"You need to take your health seriously."

"I assure you, I do."

Though Sarah didn't want Taylor to skate, his humor

inspired sinister thoughts. *I should let him skate. Let him take the risk.* The activity could sabotage his journey home. He'd never skated before, but accidents happened all the time. He'd skate like a child, potentially falling and reinjuring his spleen. And if that happened, Friday's flight would be cancelled.

"Come on, Sarah. The accident robbed me of my snowboarding goals. When can I pursue winter sports again?"

Taylor pleaded, venting. His excitement reminded her of a young boy or an adolescent, someone who desired to escape life by running outside to play. Sarah frowned. *I should let him do it.*

"Hey…" Taylor released her hand and tipped up her chin. "No sad faces."

"I was thinking." Sarah nibbled at her lip. "What about the risk?"

"Don't think. After my instructor gives me my first skating lesson, I booked a couple's massage."

"Your instructor?" When had he booked an instructor? "I didn't realize The Post Hotel employed instructors."

Taylor eyed her curiously. "Actually, it's you. Take me for a spin around the ice. You've skated before, right?"

Sarah nodded, sipping her coffee. "I'm no figure skater, but I can make my way around the ice. Whether I'm a good instructor or not, well, I'm not confident in my ability to teach."

"You'll be great," Taylor said, stretching backward. "I talked to the front desk clerk about extending our reservation. She told me the spa had a cancellation."

"After you fall, the massage will manipulate the knots, the

sore muscles." Unless an ambulance took him to Foothills Hospital.

"Hey, stop. Let's not talk about injuries. I've spent enough time at your workplace," Taylor said. "Two masseuses are coming to the cabin."

Sarah didn't respond to his outburst. "A couple's massage?"

"Well, we're a couple, yes?"

Sarah took a deep breath, then sipped the coffee. "Until Friday."

"Friday. Yes…now I understand why you're in a sour mood." Taylor slid his chair backward. "When I leave, it won't be easy on us, but can we be optimistic about the future?"

"I'm trying," Sarah said, staring at her food. "It's not offering a positive outlook."

Taylor bit into a slice of toast. A dollop of strawberry jelly coated his lips. He acted calmly while purposely messing up his face. "Life is messy. Look at me? Look at this jelly on my face? Do you still want to kiss me? Lick it off? There's a risk you could get dirty."

"Kiss you?" Sarah asked, giggling. "Yes, sounds delicious."

How could sadness and happiness squeeze her heartstrings at the same time. Sarah rose from her chair, placed her napkin on the table and went to Taylor. She peered into his eyes as she leaned forward and grasped his cheek. "Has anyone told you how special you are?"

"Nah… It's not true. I'm a simple guy. You're the special one."

Sarah climbed on his lap and kissed his lips. She didn't care who might be watching. She leaned against his forehead, clutching his face, closing her eyes. The world spun faster when they were this close. When Taylor left, how would she cope? Sarah couldn't bear to think about it.

FORTUNATELY, the hotel had skates. Dressed in winter clothing with ice skates on their feet, Sarah held tight to Taylor's hand and led him across the sidewalk to the ice surface. It glistened with potential.

Taylor smirked. "You have a strong grip, Sarah. You're squeezing the feeling out of my fingers. This could work to your advantage."

"The better to keep you on your feet. You're getting used to the boot, to walking on a blade, but go slow."

"I'm moving so slow I'm treading forward like a turtle."

"This isn't a race. Small steps until we reach the ice."

"This isn't as much fun as I thought it would be."

"Don't complain. I still have qualms about this exercise." But one glance at Taylor's face, his smile, his joy, helped Sarah discern they'd made the right decision.

"I'm excited." Taylor stepped onto the ice and wobbled.

"It's work for the teacher." Sarah braced her blade against the ice and held Taylor's free hand. No way would she let him fall. "Don't try to skate. Take time to adjust to standing on the ice."

Taylor didn't listen. He slid toward her, wobbling like a baby learning to walk. "Uh-uh. I heard you: stand in place, bend your knees."

"You're mocking me."

Taylor held tight to her hand, squeezing her fingers. "Sarah, I have excellent balance." He bent his knees, showing her what he could do. His radiant smile, his joy, amused her. A thirty-something man acting like a teenage boy. Exuberant, happy, full of life. His positive nature buoyed her spirits and she forgot to think about Friday.

"That may be, but people fall when they push forward. Skating's not walking. Don't step forward. It's best to march. Let me show you."

Sarah released Taylor's hands and skated backward, gaining some distance.

"How'd you do that?" Taylor inched toward her.

"That's a lesson for another day," Sarah said.

She taught Taylor marching steps, baby steps, slight motions, pushing outward with her feet. She faced him again. "Are you ready?"

Taylor lifted his foot slightly and marched forward, pouting. "This isn't what I expected. I'm not skating. I'm not moving fast enough. I want to glide across the ice."

Sarah sighed, her breath a puff of steam. Fast wasn't in the cards. "Okay…" She strode forward and grasped his hands. "Bend your knees. I'll pull you across the ice."

He nodded.

Sarah skated backward, pulling Taylor. She skated slowly, taking him a short distance across the ice.

"This is amazing." Taylor wobbled again. "I want to try on my own."

"Okay. But if you lose your balance, if you think you might fall, try to land on your butt, and please…not your injured side."

Taylor marched in place, taking tiny steps. He must have felt adventurous for he forced his blade into the ice and then slid. His laughter trailed across the ice with him. "Look at me... Sarah, this is awesome."

Sarah skated after him, a fall foremost on her mind. "Should we hold hands? Do you want to circle the rink with me?"

Taylor laughed. "I want to learn how to play hockey. Could you teach me?"

Sarah laughed, gliding. "Let's learn how to skate first."

"Look..." A huge smile blossomed on his face. "I'm skating."

They held hands and skated slowly around the rink. Sarah thought the lesson had gone well until Taylor wobbled a third time. His feet slid from underneath him. Instinctively, he grabbed her hand and took her down with him.

Sarah rolled onto her knees and crawled to Taylor. "Are you all right?" she asked, terrified. "Are you hurt?" She examined him, patting his abdomen, his hips.

Taylor shook his head. "Sarah," he said, grinning, pulling her close to his face. "I'm fine. I'm not hurt."

"Are you sure?"

"Stop worrying. Kiss me, Sarah." Relief suffused through her. Lying beside Taylor on the ice, not discerning the hard surface or wintry frost, she kissed him.

Sarah touched his mouth, wearing orange gloves. "Your lips are cold."

"Your cheeks are rosy. You're glowing."

"Your instructor failed you," Sarah said. "Do you want to skate more, or have you had enough exercise?"

"Another turn around the ice? If I fall a second time, you can kiss me again."

"Hmm. Is the kiss worth the risk?"

"Absolutely," Taylor said, kissing her again.

SARAH WAS grateful Taylor had booked the massage. After their brief skating adventure, they were both hurting. Taylor had fallen twice but hadn't sustained an injury. She had mixed emotions about the positive outcome. Friday's flight would happen after all.

CHAPTER EIGHTEEN

Early Monday morning, Sarah left the bathroom carrying a brush. "Do you want to leave today? The tourist spots were fabulous in Lake Louise, but I want to show you the Fairmont Banff Springs hotel. It's a world-famous castle in the mountains."

"A castle in Canada?" Taylor asked, sitting on the sofa.

"Not with turrets and towers, or royalty for that matter. It's an iconic building featuring historic architecture. If you appreciate notable designs, there's more to experience, more to do in Banff. We could shop."

"I'd like that. I need to purchase gifts for my family."

The mention of family reminded Sarah of his upcoming trip. Friday was days away and facing it meant whispering words she wasn't ready to say. *Goodbye…*

Taylor rose from the sofa. "I want to buy you a gift," Taylor said softly. "A special something to remember me by after I'm gone."

After he's gone? "That sounds final." His words stung like the distance soon to come between them. Pain pulsed beneath her breastbone. "I would *never* forget you."

"I hope not." Taylor approached her and grasped her shoulders. "Sarah…let's go back to Calgary, to your apartment. I don't care for castles in the mountains. Honestly, snowboarding and sightseeing don't appeal to me half as much as you." He looked at her expectantly. "Sarah, I don't want to get on the plane."

"I know."

"If I have to go, why not come with me?"

Hope shone in his eyes and Sarah appreciated the offer. "What do you mean, travel to Australia?"

Taylor nodded. "Sure. Why not?"

"You're serious."

"Yeah, I am." He released her. He brushed his hands through his hair. "Sarah, I'm madly in love with you."

Sarah's mouth fell open, her hand flew to her chest.

"Does my declaration of love surprise you?"

She was about to tell Taylor that traveling to Australia was impossible, but his words left her speechless. "Are you serious?" One look at his face, his brilliant blue eyes and sly half-smile, conveyed absolute sincerity. "What do I say to such a declaration?"

He grasped her shoulders. "Sarah, did you hear me? I'm in the deep end here. I need to understand your point of view. If you don't share the same feelings…"

His confession should have made her viewpoint easier to accept, easier to acknowledge. The assertion deepened their bond, but one element squeezed between them, compromising their relationship.

After his admission, how will I say goodbye?

The leaving tore at her heartstrings. "Taylor, I'm aware of my feelings. I love you, too."

He pulled her closer, studying her intently. "You do?"

"Yes, I do. I love you."

"What will we do?" he asked, grimacing.

The brush slipped from Sarah's fingers and fell to the floor, giving a distinct clunking sound. She leaned into Taylor, clutched his head in her hands and faced his worry. "We'll plan for the future."

LATER, Sarah and Taylor walked along Banff Avenue, hand in hand, passing shops lining either side of the roadway. They visited her favorite stores: Rocks & Gems, Rocky Mountain Soap, and the Banff Candy Store. Taylor bought a pandora charm for his mother, maple whiskey for his dad, and matching silver bracelets for the darlings, a term of endearment for his sister and her partner.

Sarah pointed at an art gallery. "Maybe we'll find a gift for your brother and his wife in there." Taylor purchased a stone sculpture of a wolf.

"My brother loves dogs," Taylor said. "But how will I get it home?"

"Take it in your carry on. Otherwise, you risk breaking it."

Taylor paused at the entrance of a jewelry store, staring at her in a mischievous way. "What's in this store?" He grinned, reaching for her hand. "Something special, something you might like?"

Sarah edged closer to the window display to view the modest yet exquisite samplings of gemstones; ornate rings, sparkling necklaces, and a few expensive-looking bracelets. *Nope.* She wouldn't dream of entering this store. "Seems expensive."

Taylor squeezed her fingers and urged her closer to the door. "Does the cost concern you? Money shouldn't worry you."

Sarah stepped back. "Me? Worried? I'm not worried." But Taylor was right, she was uncomfortable. With the probable cost and the manner in which the sales associate might address her. As if she couldn't afford the luxuries available for sale in this store.

"Come on, be adventurous. Come inside and peruse the inventory. We don't have to buy anything."

Sarah stood motionless on the sidewalk near the window, staring at diamond prospects that someone like her could not afford. *I can't go in there.* "You can't be serious."

Taylor pulled her nearer, hugging her, amusement creasing his eyes. "You're terrified. Why?"

"Why?" Sarah shook her head, winter winds swirled between them. "These pretty things…" Sarah pointed at the window. "I can't afford them. And it's not the kind of place I shop. They'll talk to me like a second-class citizen."

He squeezed her fingers. "I'm not convinced." Taylor laughed, opened the door, and pulled her inside the store.

"Taylor…" She gasped, but it was too late. She stood inside the store facing showcases of luxury.

An Asian salesclerk greeted them. "Welcome. If there's anything I can help you with or items you'd like to see, please let me know."

"We'll do that." Taylor nodded.

He pulled her toward the showcase and she reluctantly walked toward it. The store carried exquisite pieces. Sunshine streamed through the front windows, casting light on a showcase glistening with red and green Aurora gemstones. *This isn't happening. Taylor isn't purchasing sentimental jewels from this place.* No boyfriend, especially at this point in a relationship, would make such a commitment, at least not in her experience. "We're just looking," Sarah said. Despite misgivings, she inched closer to the case as if yearning to own a brilliant gemstone. Glamorous diamond rings, glittering jewels sending charismatic light in various directions. Sarah shouldn't covet one, but she craved such a gem, wanting one on her finger…someday.

Not today.

"Hey." Taylor leaned toward her as if he had a secret to tell, then nudged her toward the case and said, "I see the way you're looking at these beauties. I'm making your dreams come true. I'm buying you one." He addressed the clerk, "I want to purchase a promise ring for my girlfriend."

"What?" Sarah gasped, shocked. *His girlfriend? A promise ring?* What did he mean to promise?

"It's okay, Sarah. Let me do this."

"What do you have in mind?" the salesclerk asked.

"I'm from Australia."

"Ah, I wondered. Given the accent, I guessed either Australia or the UK."

"My enunciation gives me away every time," Taylor said. "You wouldn't happen to have any Australian opals?"

"I do." The clerk approached another showcase. She grabbed a set of keys from her pocket and opened the case. She placed a tray of rings on top of the glass counter. "There's three, maybe four opal rings."

"Can you show them to us?"

Sarah approached the showcase then froze, immobile, like the wolf sculpture Taylor had bought for his brother. She listened to the conversation, having a difficult time believing a ring purchase was in the making. Taylor wanted to give her a promise ring. Why?

"You're terrified. Come closer, Sarah."

She didn't move.

"Sarah, is something wrong?"

She fingered Taylor's forearm. "You don't have to do this. You don't have to make promises to me." And honestly, she didn't want a token of his affection if he couldn't keep those promises.

"I want to. It's important to me."

"Okay." Sarah took a shaky breath and moved closer to the showcase. The clerk pulled a ring from the tray. The opal was not a diamond, but it sparkled in a similar way.

"This gemstone has been waiting for someone special." The clerk eyed Sarah, a whimsical smile on her face. "It has amazing clarity. It's an opal solitaire with an heirloom cut, set in a band of yellow gold. The stone is free of blemishes and has five small diamonds on either side of the opal." She looked at Sarah. "I'm not sure what your budget is, but this ring would make an adequate promise ring."

"How much is it?" Sarah asked.

The salesclerk examined a small white tag.

"Don't tell her," Taylor said. "The cost is between the buyer and the seller."

Sarah sighed. "Then maybe the buyer should review the purchase first."

When the clerk passed the ring to Taylor, he accepted it. Sarah watched him studying its magnificence before facing her. "Don't worry about the cost, sweetheart. All gifts have their price and this one is worth any price." He held the ring closer to himself, studying it intently, then looked at her with a serene smile. "It's beautiful, Sarah. Sophisticated, like you." He passed it to her. "What do you think? Do you like it?"

Amazed, Sarah held the ring and studied it intimately. An ample-sized opal, pearlescent white and at least half a carat. When the light struck it, it gleamed. "It's beautiful."

"Put it on your finger," Taylor said. "Let's see if it fits."

Sarah slid the ring on her finger, her ring finger. It fit perfectly. Taylor watched her stretching her fingers, pondering the magnificence. Something she'd always wanted for herself but had never bought. No one had given her such a gift.

The clerk interjected, saying, "This is the best part of my job. Assisting couples in love always makes me smile."

"Are we that obvious?" Taylor asked.

"Well, it's difficult to hide love. It shines on your faces. How did you meet?"

Taylor shrugged. "I had an accident at Sunshine Village Ski Resort. I met Sarah at the hospital."

Sarah was listening to the conversation, or at least trying

to, but the gorgeous ring on her finger overwhelmed her. Though she said, "I'm his nurse. I mean, I was his nurse."

"That's the most romantic and painful story I've ever heard."

Sarah eyed the salesclerk. "He's still healing, but please don't tell anyone. I'm violating my professional ethics. I don't want to lose my job."

The clerk dismissed the statement with a wave of her hand. "Couples meet in different ways all the time. I wouldn't let a matter like *ethics* get in the way of true love. Years from now you'll have a great story to share with your kids, your grandkids if you're blessed."

"Depends how much of a promise this guy makes." Sarah shook her head, rolling her eyes. "He hasn't bought the ring yet."

Taylor laughed. "Do you like it?" Taylor asked.

Do I like it? It's a ring. Brilliant stones held in a band of yellow gold, and though she lusted for this treasure, the clarity didn't hold half as much fascination as the guy standing next to her, the one who wanted to purchase the precious gem. She wouldn't hurt him by saying no.

"I love it. I'm not taking it off my finger." *Ever.* "So Taylor, I hope you're as serious about the gift as you are about your promise."

Taylor smiled, whispering, "You're pulling at my heartstrings. Sarah, you were meant to own the ring." He looked at the clerk and said louder, "We'll take it."

Sarah gave him a face. "Don't be absurd. You don't understand."

"What do you need to make you more comfortable?"

"Well, the price?"

"The cost doesn't matter." Taylor reached for her hand and studied the ring on her finger. "I like this ring. It suits you. And you said it yourself; you love it." Taylor pulled his wallet from his jacket pocket, retrieved his credit card and passed it to the clerk.

The clerk didn't rush to the cash register as Sarah would have expected. She studied them adoringly. "I love your story as much as I love your impulsiveness." She giggled. "I want to do something for you. You didn't ask for a price break, but how about twenty percent off the purchase price?"

"We'd be grateful," Taylor said. "That's kind of you."

"You're welcome. Always happy to help." The clerk finalized the transaction. "Do you want to wear it?"

"I'm never taking it off." Sarah looked at Taylor. "Thank you. Your thoughtfulness means the world to me. I'll remember this moment for the rest of my life."

LATER AT A MEXICAN EATERY, Magpie & Stump, Sarah sipped a mango margarita. She eyed her hand often, unable to look away from the ring. The opal caught the light, the diamonds sparkled. No man had *ever* given her such an amazing gift. She'd had several relationships over the years. She'd compared past boyfriends and past disappointments to Taylor, but no man had put a ring on her finger. She never wanted to take it off.

"You like it?" Taylor asked.

Sarah raised her hand and looked at the ring for what

seemed like the hundredth time, still surprised it hugged her finger. "Honey, I love it. I appreciate your thoughtfulness."

Taylor smiled serenely, then sipped the cerveza. "Yet there's curiosity in your eyes. Do you want to ask me something?"

He was perceptive. Sarah sipped her margarita then looked directly at Taylor. "Okay. Here it goes. What are you promising? What's the real reason you gave me the ring?"

Taylor placed the beer on the table and reached for her hand. "For one, it's an Australian opal, so it'll remind you of Australia. And more importantly, I don't want you to forget me." A seriousness in his eyes proclaimed his sentiment.

"I won't forget you. How could I after everything we've shared."

"I don't know. Look at this place."

Sarah looked around the rustic restaurant but all she saw was a busy establishment, occupied tables with guests; families with children, couples like them. "What about this place?"

Taylor waved his hand as if pointing. "The Canadian men. When I disappear from your life, what if you meet one, what if you forget you ever met me?"

Sarah took a deep breath. She'd had her fill of fishy men and the question of citizenship had never been part of her concern. Maybe it should have been. They'd disappointed her. Let her down. No Canadian boy had been willing to make a commitment.

"I only see you, Taylor Quinn. *You* are the only man who matters to me."

Taylor squeezed her fingers. His eyes brightened. "Your

eyes are firing with passion, like you're pleading a point. You mean it, don't you?"

"Every word."

Taylor fingered his beer glass. "The Australian opal is known for love and passion, and we've had a fondness for each other from the start. I have feelings for you, I'm attracted to you, and serious about our relationship. Certain commitments are important to me. Maybe not a marriage commitment. Not yet. As a couple we have not matured enough."

Sarah nodded. "I understand."

Taylor stretched forward. "Sarah, do you want a stronger promise? Is the opal not enough for you?" He seemed serious. Too serious. Sarah didn't want Taylor to think she wasn't grateful.

"I appreciate your generosity. No one else has given me a gift like this."

"But it isn't enough."

"Maybe. After all, our relationship is new. This isn't the right time to discuss wedding gowns and spoken vows, but yes. Eventually, I want more."

He sniffed, clearly worried. "I don't frighten easily. Name your price."

"Really?"

Taylor stared at her fixedly, like he was preparing to do whatever it took to please her. Sarah couldn't believe it. She had to respond in kind. She said, "Remember, you encouraged this confession, so I hope you're prepared to pay the price. I. Want. You. It's a big ask. However, let friendship be our promise, for now."

CHAPTER NINETEEN

Sarah's declaration of love hit the spot like Cupid's arrow gliding straight into his heart.

She loves me? She wants me?

He'd dated many women, and most had wanted similar assurances, but for one reason or another the partnerships had always soured, causing a parting of the ways. This time seemed different as Sarah appreciated their relationship, and more importantly, him.

Her honesty earned his respect. After the declaration, he only desired to hold her hand and take her to a private place. A domicile where two people could forge a life together while mitigating the complications.

If she'd asked him to meet her at the altar to declare their wedding vows, he'd likely have done it. He was that much in love. He'd return to Banff Jewels and buy a new ring, a band ornamented with a diamond, a stone larger than the first promise.

Instead, he'd suggested they get a room at the castle in the mountains and Sarah had agreed. Later that afternoon, they checked in at the luxurious Fairmont Banff Springs.

They indulged in Afternoon Tea in the Rundle lounge, overlooking the scenic wonder of Mount Rundle. Yet another thoughtful, peaceful experience, but this time without jelly candying his face.

After, given the winter weather, they explored the inside of the hotel. From the grand staircase to the Spanish Walk, they explored every facet of the archeological masterpiece. Sarah's face brightened when they entered Mount Stephen Hall.

"This is my favorite room in the castle," she said, preceding him into the hall. "I always come here." She looked at him, her eyes glistening. "If I were a rich woman, I'd get married in this place."

"Good to know. Gives me time to get my finances in order," Taylor said. He imagined Sarah dressed in white, a gown suitable for a princess. If he were a rich man, he'd choose such an event space himself. The medieval atmosphere appealed to his historic self. Limestone floors, stone walls and large buttress windows allowed in ample light. Candle sconces on the walls and candelabras on the ceiling at least two storeys above their heads. "I see why you adore this chamber."

Decorated for Christmas, evergreen garlands with red poinsettias and red bows hugged the limestone archways. The Christmas tree, nearly twenty-four feet high, decked the hall with poinsettia garlands, red and gold ornaments and golden lanterns, gilt and glitter precisely set into the branches.

It was a sight to see, and they took a selfie in front of the decorated fir tree, but Sarah held his attention.

"When I enter this hall, I stand higher, like a princess," Sarah said. "Named after the first president of the Canadian Pacific Railway, this room whispers history."

"It's probably haunted."

Sarah's eyebrows rose. "Well actually…in the late 1920s a bride died on her wedding day. She fell on a marble staircase."

Not the picture Taylor had imagined. "I prefer to focus on happier outcomes. If this hall had been built in Great Britain, regal affairs would have taken place here." They were alone in the hall. Taylor grasped Sarah's hand and urged her closer to him.

"Yes, magnificent occasions," Sarah said, her eyes lit with possibility. "Grand balls, royal teas, maybe a celebrity's posh wedding?"

Taylor held Sarah closer, breathing her vanilla perfume. "Your face lights up when you speak of marrying. My lady, we could flourish in a place such as this." He stepped away and gave her a gallant bow. "I'm not a prince, mind you. I'm not dignified enough for the lordship. No, I'd be the knight fighting to protect your honor on the battlefield."

Sarah giggled. She reached for his hand and pulled him to her. "Oh? Tell me about it."

He moved into first position and held Sarah's hand. She twirled, initiating the first steps of the waltz. "I'd sweep you off your feet, dance with you, and after…hoist you onto my noble steed. We'd depart the castle. You'd accompany me on exciting adventures."

Sarah froze. "When I live in the lap of luxury, in all things grand and beautiful, you'd remove me from this regal place, stealing me away from everything I've known?"

"I'd hope you'd come with me, willingly."

A pensive look cooled her excitement. Not a smile, not quite a frown. "If your steed is sure-footed, I'll consider it. But where would you take me?"

Good question. Where would he take his princess? Taylor knew where he'd like to travel. Across the ocean to the lands of Australia, to Sydney. But she was right. Removing a woman from her known territory, a city, a family, her home, felt wrong.

"Where would you have me go? Castles in other provinces with medieval nostalgia? Other continents?" Sarah asked, frowning. "Perhaps a country warmer than this one."

Sarah clutched his hand. She studied him seriously, her eyes shrouded with questions he couldn't answer. All he knew for sure was one of them had to make a sacrifice. *Who?*

"I'd like to visit Sydney," Sarah said finally.

"Ah, my love, there's no grander place. Plenty of beaches to soak up the sun. You could lie on your lounge chair with a courtier fanning your fragile-looking skin."

"I'm not fragile." Sarah shrugged, smirking. "Hmm. Not likely." The magic dissipated as quickly as it had appeared. Tiny crease lines puckered her brow. She stepped away from him. The castle and their mindset now forgotten in preference to present-day times.

"Where do you live, Taylor? We have not talked about it."

He took her hand and led her toward the exit. "A studio apartment near Freshwater Beach. A block and a half from the ocean."

"The place where you surf?"

"Yes. Either there or at Manly."

"I'd like to see it. I could visit you."

Taylor pulled Sarah into his arms again. He kissed her forehead. He wanted to kiss her lips. "If you love me as much as you say you do, you'll come."

"I can't accept that you're leaving, Taylor."

"It's not easy on me either."

CHAPTER TWENTY

Friday brought a tempest of emotions. Sarah wasn't prepared for Taylor's flight to Vancouver, let alone the fourteen-hour jaunt to Sydney, to Australia. The journey would carry him so far into blue skies she worried she might never see him again.

How would the distance affect them?

Their relationship was new. Could they bear the space between them?

She'd taken a huge risk by bringing Taylor into her life. Their relationship violated hospital rules, ethical and moral values. She could lose her job.

Now what?

Turmoil flowed through her veins, the idea of him leaving giving her a pounding headache. The aching behind her eyes, eyes swollen from crying. She'd cried herself to sleep last night, quietly, unbeknownst to Taylor who had lain beside her, holding her, stroking her skin, her ribs, the side of her breast, without speaking. What could he say? What could she say? The silence had been deafening. At times, she'd wondered if he'd wept as well.

They drove onward, like silent sentinels, coming closer and closer to their fate, to Calgary International Airport. Neither were ready to say goodbye.

She glanced at Taylor and though he gave her a weak smile, she saw his emotions were as fragile as hers. His face scrunched, his lips lifted and fell without speaking. What was he thinking? It seemed like he might cry and if he lost so much as a single tear, she'd lose it.

Sarah took a deep, cleansing breath. Best to distract herself, and him. "What will you do when you get home?"

Taylor wasn't quick in responding. He scratched his head, searching for something beyond the passenger window, tapping his fingers against the armrest while watching passing vehicles. "Who cares. Abandon my suitcase by the door? Leave my snowboard in the middle of the living area." He glanced at Sarah, his eyes as red as hers. "I'll think about you…and everything I left behind. You're—a sweetheart of a woman. I'll ask myself the same question repeatedly…"

"What's that?"

"Have I made the biggest mistake of my life?"

Sarah sighed. She'd be asking herself similar questions, but sharing regrets during a sensitive time wouldn't help either of them cope with saying goodbye. "Will you go to the ocean? Will the water comfort you?"

"Maybe. According to my family the weather's been unusually hot, nearly forty degrees Celsius." He looked at her. "The apartment will be hotter than a sauna, soulless, too. I might as well escape to the beach and take a dip. Drown my sorrow."

Sarah changed lanes, imagining Taylor on the beach, wishing she was traveling with him. "A swim? Not a surf?"

"A quick run in and out. I'll be tired, jet-lagged after the flight." Taylor glanced at her. "What about you? You'll have your place to yourself?"

"But no one to prepare my bath." Her face fell. Having her condo to herself? If only he knew how lonely and depressed her life would feel without him. The condo would be no more than an empty room, holding nothing worthwhile but cherished memories, rooms silent and foreboding without someone special to talk to, to share life's stories with, to dance...

"Before I met you," Sarah said, "I didn't grasp what it felt like to have someone special in my life. I liked what was happening between us."

"You make it sound like it's over. We're not done. We're not finished."

Sarah gripped the steering wheel tighter. Maybe he was right. Maybe he was wrong. Only time would tell if distance would break them apart or pull them together. This worried Sarah. She frowned. She didn't want Taylor to leave but she wouldn't beg him to stay either.

"It won't be the same...without you," Sarah said, her voice faltering. She willed herself not to cry, willing restraint, to let Taylor depart with her dignity intact.

He sighed. He touched her leg. "Sarah, we don't have much time. We need to address some issues before we get to the airport."

"Say what's on your mind. If I say too much, I'll lose it."

"I hate this. I hate that I'm leaving you."

"I don't like it either."

"I don't want to go. Do you understand how difficult it is to leave? To pack my bags? To abandon the most important woman I've *ever* met?"

"Why am I driving you to the airport? It's the worst kind of torture. If I was an adventurous woman, like the man sitting next to me, I'd turn this car around and steal you home." She knew she couldn't do it, but she wanted to.

Taylor gave a brief puff of laughter. "I wouldn't lift a finger to stop you," Taylor said seriously. "I'm leaving my best friend. I mean, we haven't known each other for long, but there's no doubt in my mind…you're my partner. So, what do we do?" he asked, staring at her, stroking her leg. "Your home's in Canada. My home's in Australia. How do we breach the distance to build one home together? That is, if you want to build a future with me."

Sarah shook her head. "It's too much to think about right now. I suppose one of us has to change, one of us has to relocate, but who has the courage?"

"That's the million-dollar question. My parents are older."

Sarah reflected on her family; her parents, her sister and brother, not to mention her friends. If she relocated, how would the distance affect them? Affect her relationship with them? "I'd have to quit my job." Sarah shook her head. "One of us has to leave someone they love for our relationship to continue."

Taylor sighed. "Maybe we don't have to decide yet. I want

some sort of plan, some hope for the future, before I exit your car."

"Me, too."

"Sarah, come to Australia," Taylor said, his tone insistent and firm. "Maybe we don't have to decide today. I'm only suggesting this because I've seen your Canada. You might want to relocate, but how can you decide without visiting my country? You might love Australia. Please, tell me you'll come."

Taylor's eyes shone with yearning, a confident appeal that compelled her to say, "Yes. Maybe. It's a long flight."

"If you agree to come over, I'll pay the flight cost. Please?"

Sarah nodded. Tears filled her eyes, making it difficult to see the roadway. She wiped the liquid away, trying to smile. "I'll come, but it will take some planning. I don't know when."

He stroked her thigh. "That's good enough for me. For now."

AFTER TAYLOR LEFT, Sarah bought a Tim Hortons coffee and drove to the Edward H. LaBorde Airplane Watching Area. She climbed out of her car consumed with anxiety, feeling somber, distressed, barely able to stand on her feet. She stumbled to a nearby bench, feeling numb.

She sipped her coffee, remembering their final goodbyes at the departure level. They'd embraced, with Taylor massaging her arm, caressing her face, wiping away the tears. She'd been crying so hard she could barely speak. Taylor's eyes had been teary as well. He'd hugged her firmly, trying to kiss away the falling tears.

"I love you, Sarah." Those four simple yet significant words encouraged sorrow, sorrow for every joyful moment that was now left in limbo.

Helplessness consumed her. Why was she sitting on this bench, this hard bench, feeling sorry for herself? Feeling numb. Blank. And not taking steps to remedy the situation?

She needed to swim!

What was wrong with her? Why hadn't she purchased an airline ticket and accompanied Taylor to Australia? She'd made excuses: job, family, her apartment.

Sarah! Snap out of it. You wouldn't be depressed if you'd taken a risk.

Sarah watched plane after plane lift into the sky and the tears eased with each passing aircraft. When Air Canada Flight 213 rose into the blue, her heart broke. She knew Taylor was on *that* plane. She felt him deep in her heart: painful throbbing, breathing difficulties. The plane rose, higher and higher, taking the man who could be, no was…the love of her life.

What am I doing here? Watching the love of my life…fly away. What's wrong with me? I should be with him on that plane. Swim, Sarah, Swim…

Rising from the bench, Sarah carried her Tim Hortons coffee. She hurried across the gravel. "Oh God." She cried loudly, stumbling, falling to her knees and scraping her skin. *This is too much.* Sarah ignored the pain and rose to her feet, hurrying to her car, then grasped the door handle and searched the skies for the departing plane. It had flown a considerable distance. Now no more than a dot in the sky.

The separation was unbearable. She'd never been good at negotiating relationships, but maybe this one was worth the risk. If she loved Taylor, a man from Sydney, Australia, she needed to act. And fast.

CHAPTER TWENTY-ONE

When the wheels lifted off the ground and the plane rocketed into the sky, Taylor closed his eyes and took a deep breath. Normally, he liked the feeling of the aircraft speeding along the runway; the thrust upward, the roar of the engine, the birdlike rush of leaving the ground and flying into the air.

Not today.

As the ground shifted farther and farther away, the only individual who held significant meaning in his life was the woman he'd left behind. Sarah—

I'm a dumb ass.

He pulled the window shade down, not wanting to see the ground, or even admit to himself the treasure he'd left behind. He hated this emotion. Though this decision was made for good reasons, traveling home rankled a place deep inside his soul. Instinctively, he knew: *Sarah is my home.*

What have I done? He'd left her. Left his home. There was

no home without Sarah. Injury or no injury, he'd made the biggest mistake of his life.

Taylor sighed, settling in for the flight. He pulled the window shade up, in time to see a wondrous view of the mountains. He was leaving them, too.

CHAPTER TWENTY-TWO

The tears stopped falling now that Sarah had a plan. She drove, clutching the steering wheel the entire ride, determined to take the fastest route home: Airport Trail, Deerfoot Trail, McKnight Boulevard to the Trans-Canada Highway. Forty-five minutes later she walked through the front door of her condo. By this time, Taylor had flown more than halfway to Vancouver.

Time, not much time to catch up with him.

Sarah dropped her purse on the floor and sank to the sofa. Nerves pulsated through her head and butterflies flittered in her thoughts. She swept her fingers through her hair, pulling the strands away from her eyes.

What if I can't find a flight?

Afflicted with yearning and nervous energy, Sarah's fingers quivered while downloading the Air Canada Flight App into her cell phone, all the while worrying flights might not be available. And then…an option appeared on the screen: 7:50

p.m. departure from Calgary to Vancouver, and fortunately, seats were still available on the midnight leg to Sydney.

Sarah clapped her hands, eager and raring to go. She was excited about this trip, about seeing Taylor again. Tears sprang into her eyes, but these were tears of happiness.

I'm traveling to Sydney! Look out, Taylor, here I come.

She concentrated on the work, soon addressing the staggering flight cost, a whopping two thousand dollars, but no expense could deter true love. When she found her sweetheart in Vancouver, Taylor would be surprised to see her. Sarah smiled, thinking about her boyfriend, her lover, and the moment they would come face to face. Licking her lips, she selected the flight, booking a one-way ticket to Sydney. A traveler's VISA came soon after.

Now it was time to retrieve her suitcase and pack.

What will I take with me?

Sarah giggled, smiling, contemplating the tangerine bikini, summer dresses, and Taylor. She threw her suitcase on the bed and packed essentials: T-shirts, jeans, her favorite beach dresses, pajamas, and underwear. A few bathing suits for sunning herself or swimming in the ocean. She imagined the waves curling to shore. Breathing deeply, she closed her eyes momentarily.

Maybe Taylor would keep his promise and teach her to surf. If she let him.

Sarah couldn't get over it, she was traveling to Sydney, Australia. She couldn't wait to see Taylor's surprised face. This spurred her into action. She didn't have much time to return to the airport.

With her suitcase packed, Sarah collected final items: her

passport, purse, cell phone, laptop, cords, and then called for a taxi. When it arrived, she glanced at her home one final time. She loved this condo, this home, but without Taylor the building might as well have been an empty shell.

A home's worth held less value if Taylor wasn't part of it. Why hadn't this occurred to her sooner?

Taylor is my home. My heart, my soulmate, my everything. Home is wherever I'm with you…I'm traveling home.

Sarah couldn't wait to reach him.

Enroute to the airport, she texted:

I'm coming, Taylor. Wait for me. I'm boarding the 7:50 p.m. flight out of Calgary. Don't leave YVR without me.

CHAPTER TWENTY-THREE

In the backseat of a taxi, Sarah watched the cabbie gazing at her via the rearview mirror. The infrequent ogling rattled her nerves, contributing to her anxiety. Though the occasional glance likely arose from curiosity, she crossed her arms, frowning, and clutched her cell phone tighter.

Calm yourself, Sarah. It's the journey worrying you, not the driver. And maybe the impending phone call. She hadn't told her family about Taylor. They didn't know about this trip.

Oh my god, when Mom learns the truth, what will she say?

It didn't matter what her mother thought, whether she scolded her or begged her to stay in the country. Sarah could not leave without notifying her family.

But there's no privacy in this car, he's staring at me… the driver will hear my story. A threat of appearing impulsive and foolish. Sarah gripped her phone tighter, preparing for the unavoidable lecture. Still, facing judgment and embarrassment seemed better than worrying her family when they couldn't reach her.

Sarah sighed, unlocked the screen, and pressed the phone icon. Choosing Favorites, she stared at her mother's image. *Oh, Mom— What will you think? That I'm having another relationship crisis?* Sarah inhaled deeply then pressed her mother's image and waited for the call to connect.

"Hi, Sarah. It's good to hear from you."

"Mom, we need to talk," Sarah mumbled, her voice strangled, quiet and weak.

"I don't like your tone," her mother said slowly. "What's wrong?"

Sarah swallowed, peering at the driver. She couldn't put anything past her mom. She always knew when complicating factors waylaid her daughter's life. "What I'm about to say will surprise you."

Her mom breathed into the receiver. "Tell me, Sarah. I'm always here for you."

She took a shaky breath. "I'm on the way to the airport."

"Oh? Why? Where are you going?"

Sarah peered at passing cars, mindful the taxi driver was watching her, listening to her conversation. "Sydney, Australia."

Mom gasped.

"I realize how this sounds," Sarah said, closing her eyes, waiting for the judgment, her mother's opinion, an emotional outburst even the forthcoming lecture. *Taylor*—She should have acknowledged their relationship. Her family should have met him weeks ago. No time to share Taylor with her family.

The excuses didn't change the situation, but the timing hadn't been right for introductions.

"Have you been planning this trip, or is it last minute? It's surprising hearing about it now."

"I couldn't tell you sooner."

"Why not?"

"No time."

Mom sighed. "I can't believe you're traveling let alone making your way to the airport."

"I'm sorry, Mom," Sarah replied anxiously. "This was a last-minute decision."

"You're facing something," Mom said. "Sarah, I'm worried. It isn't like you to make rash decisions. What's wrong? Are you okay?"

"I've met someone." The hardest and easiest disclosure of her life.

Silence on the other end of the receiver as her mother reflected on the news. "What's his name? Did you find him on the Internet? Are you traveling to Australia to meet this man in person?"

Sarah disregarded her mother's carefully controlled tone. "His name's Taylor Quinn. He's not a stranger and this is not an Internet date. We met a few weeks ago at work."

"Oh, I see."

Sarah explained how she met Taylor, the snowboarding accident, his stay on Unit 44, his recovery, and how Taylor had been forced to travel home. It was problematic explaining the part about Taylor being her patient. "Mom, I know how crazy this sounds, and I'm sorry to break this news to you so suddenly, but I need your support. I can't face life without him." Her voice quivered.

Her mother sighed on the other end of the phone. "Sarah, this decision to travel to another country seems rash. Hasty. I'm having a difficult time processing all you've told me, but I am sensitive to your feelings."

"I appreciate that."

"Do you?" her mother asked, expressing concern. "Do you love this man?"

Sarah took a deep breath, her eyes filling with tears. More than anything, she wanted her mother's support. "I love him," she said, rasping the words.

"Aw, Sarah… While I'm surprised, I understand. I really do. Darling daughter, this trip concerns me. I'm worried about you. If I asked you to forget your plans, forget this flight, what would you say?"

"I'd ask you to support me…to accept I can't be without Taylor," Sarah said. "I need to go. He left early this afternoon. He's left a hole in my heart."

"Okay, you're emotional. My advice won't change your mind?"

"I need your support, not your advice," Sarah said.

"How do I respond to that?" Sarah didn't speak while waiting for her mother's response. She said, "You're in a taxi on the way to the airport, on the way to who knows what, but this isn't about me. It's about you. I do support *you*."

"I'm almost at the airport."

"Sarah, I understand I can't change your mind, so will you do me one favor?"

"Yes… Maybe."

"Let me know when you've arrived safely in Australia and where you'll be staying."

"I'll inform you, I promise. I'll text Taylor's phone number, so you have a point of reference."

"That's great. That's a start. May I suggest something else?"

"You might as well. You will without my prompting anyway."

"I can't believe I'm about to say this," Mom said, heaving a sigh. "Send me a picture of you, sweet daughter, holding a koala bear. I've always wanted to hold a koala bear."

Sarah gasped, laughing through her tears. She couldn't understand why she was crying again. She had least expected her mother's support. "How will you explain this to Dad, to Ali and Shawn?"

"I'll tell them the truth. They'd expect no less." Then Mom laughed. "Hopefully, your siblings don't follow you on the next flight."

"It's something they'd do," Sarah said, laughing. "I love you, Mom."

"I love you more."

Sarah heaved a sigh. "I need to say goodbye."

"One more thing."

"I have to go," Sarah replied. "I'm close to the airport."

"I was about to say," Mom said, her tone serious. "Your family should meet your new friend. And…Safe travels, Sarah."

"Bye, Mom."

After Sarah paid the taxi driver, he climbed out of the bright yellow Prius and reached into the trunk for her suitcase. It was large. Heavy. Yet he lifted the case with ease and placed it on the asphalt.

"*As Salaam Alaykum*, peace be upon you," he said, regarding her in a thoughtful way.

"Thank you," Sarah replied, not knowing how to respond.

"My apologies if I've made you uncomfortable," he said, rolling the suitcase to the curb. "I heard your story, pieces of it anyway. You're brave. They say the journey of a thousand miles begins with a single step."

Sarah looked at the ground. The cabbie gave her an earnest look; it was difficult facing his advice.

"We're not acquainted so I shouldn't be asking this," Sarah said, glancing upward shyly. "Am I making the right decision?"

"Only you can answer that, though your heart wouldn't lead you in the wrong direction."

Sarah nodded, mindful of his words. The inspiring remark gave her the strength to carry on with her plans.

"Have a safe trip, ma'am." He smiled then and climbed into his Checker Cab.

Sarah watched the vehicle drive away while pressing her phone into a purse slung around her body, then she grasped her suitcase and walked toward the airport door. Glass double doors slid open and she passed through the entry, determined to fly toward her future.

CHAPTER TWENTY-FOUR

Sarah checked in for her Air Canada flight and then passed through the Security Checkpoint with relative ease, arriving at Gate C55 by 7:00 p.m. The electronic display monitor indicated the flight would board at 7:30 p.m. She'd be on her way soon.

Sarah found a seat in the waiting area, retrieved her phone from her purse and unlocked the screen, searching for text messages from Taylor.

Why haven't I heard from him? He doesn't know I'm traveling.

She texted: "I'm at the gate. The plane boards in thirty minutes. Where are you?"

No response.

Hmm. What does this mean?

Fifteen minutes later, a flight attendant spoke into the loudspeaker: "This is a flight notification for all passengers traveling on Air Canada Flight 225 to Vancouver. Unfortunately, the flight has been delayed due to a maintenance issue. We're addressing the situation as quickly as we can, and as soon as me know more, we'll advise. Thank you for your understanding and for choosing Air Canada."

What? A horrible feeling settled in her gut. An unnerving feeling. A flight delay could threaten her goal of meeting Taylor. What if the issue couldn't be resolved? What if the flight was cancelled? She did the math, the hours, mindful of the connecting flight to Sydney. It didn't depart until midnight, Vancouver time.

Calm down, Sarah. There's plenty of time to catch the Sydney flight.

But one hour later at 8:15 p.m., still no word on whether the flight would leave. As the minutes passed, her anxiety rose. Sarah glanced at the monitor frequently, hoping the notice board notification would change to *Boarding Soon*. The board remained blank. She glanced at her phone, gripping it tightly.

Still no word from Taylor.

She scrutinized passengers in the immediate area, listening to snippets of conversation. *What's wrong with the plane? We should have heard an update by now. If the flight doesn't leave soon, we'll miss the connection!*

Sarah clutched her forehead and closed her eyes. *This can't be happening!* The longer the wait the faster her blood rushed through her veins. If the situation didn't improve, she was certain she'd succumb to illness. She rose from her seat and paced toward the counter.

"Can I help you?" the agent asked.

"What's happening with the flight," Sarah asked. "I have to get to Vancouver tonight."

The agent frowned. "You and everyone else in the waiting area. I was about to give passengers an update. I'm sorry. I've been advised by the flight crew that Flight 225 has been cancelled."

"Cancelled?" Sarah gasped. "This can't be happening." Her face flushed. Her head hurt. "What do I do now?" she asked, swallowing. "I have to get to Vancouver. Tonight!"

"Yes, I understand."

"How can you? I have a connecting flight, I have…" Sarah said, her voice rising, tears threatening. "Well, I can't miss it."

"My apologies for the inconvenience, ma'am. You'll need to speak to a customer representative to rebook the flight. You'll find Air Canada Customer Service near Gate 51."

"No," Sarah said, feeling exasperated. "I need help. I'll face a lineup of passengers, and with my luck, no seats will be available by the time I reach the area. You don't understand." Sarah bordered on hysteria. "My boyfriend's flying to Sydney tonight. I'm supposed to join him." Sarah's voice broke. "I haven't been able to contact him. He doesn't know I'm coming."

"One moment, ma'am." The flight attendant focused on the computer screen. "Though I can't rebook your flight, seats are still available on the nine-thirty flight to Vancouver. It's the last departure this evening." She smiled in reassurance. "Don't worry, you'll make it."

"I wish I had your confidence."

"If you hurry to the customer service area you won't need to stand in line or speak to a representative. Scan your boarding pass at the kiosk. A new boarding pass will print for the next available departure to Vancouver."

With this information Sarah should have been relieved, but the anxiety only rose. "Where do I go?"

The agent pointed off to her right. "The Air Canada Customer Service area near Gate 51. Use the kiosk. What's your boyfriend's name?"

"Taylor."

The attendant looked at Sarah. "Seriously, he has no knowledge that you're meeting him?"

"No." Sarah shook her head. "It's a long, complicated story. I've texted him but maybe there's a problem with his phone. He hasn't replied."

"I can tell you're worried. Maybe I can help. What's his last name?"

"Quinn, Taylor Quinn."

"I'll try and get a message to the agent in Vancouver that someone special will be joining Taylor. If the message doesn't get through to him, you'll be a nice surprise for your boyfriend. Have a good flight, Sarah. All my best to you and Taylor."

"I appreciate your kindness. Thank you so much."

Sarah left the gate and made her way to the kiosk. She scanned her boarding pass and the machine printed a new one. When Sarah knew she was confirmed on the 9:30 p.m. flight, she breathed a sigh of relief. Hopefully, Flight AC227 would depart on time.

The flight was scheduled to leave from the same gate, so Sarah returned to the waiting area and took a seat. Around 8:45 p.m., the agent spoke into the microphone: "Sarah

Evans, please come to the podium."

Fearing the worst, Sarah rose from her seat and approached the agent, twisting the ring on her finger. "Please tell me the plane's leaving on time?"

"Everything's okay. We work hard to meet our passengers' needs but can't always control issues that arise during air travel. Miss Evans, when your earlier flight was cancelled, I sensed your frustration. I wanted to correct the situation as best I could. I hope this news pleases you: I changed your seat assignment on the flight to Sydney."

"Really?" Sarah couldn't believe it. "That's generous." She could have lost control of her emotions in that moment as the agent's kindness meant she'd be able sit beside Taylor. She pictured herself with him and the idea of togetherness eased her anxiety.

The agent smiled. "Now you'll be sitting beside Taylor." She pressed closer and whispered, "No one wants to sit at the rear of the plane. Those toilets…they're constantly flushing."

Sarah laughed. "You're amazing. How do I thank you?"

"Given the trouble you've experienced tonight, it's the least I could do."

Sarah sighed. "You don't know the half of it. I really appreciate your assistance."

"Honey, it's an absolute pleasure to add joy to someone's life. I hope you have a good flight." The agent pressed a gift card into her hand. "We're giving passengers random acts of kindness and you're the perfect candidate. Please accept this gift and get yourself a latte from Starbucks. You could use a coffee. You have a long night ahead of you."

Sarah accepted the gift. She stood near the podium,

holding the card in her hands, grateful, not knowing what to say. "Thank you so much."

"Have a good flight, Sarah. Say hello to Mr. Australia for me."

Sarah said a final thank you and then walked to Starbucks where she bought a chestnut praline latte and a gingerbread loaf. After sitting near the gate, she retrieved her phone. Taylor still hadn't replied to her text message.

Taylor, I hope you haven't deactivated your phone…

Whatever the reason for his lack of response, it didn't matter. She'd find him in Vancouver, in the waiting area or on the plane.

CHAPTER TWENTY-FIVE

Damn it! The brutal *thwack* upset him. While reaching for his phone from the bin in security it had slipped from his fingers, crashing to the airport floor. He'd retrieved it, hoping it was okay, but the screen had shattered into a million little pieces. Viewing anything on it was next to impossible. How would he get a message to Sarah or respond to hers? His phone had dinged twice, but he couldn't read the screen. And to make matters worse…the phone died. There probably wasn't any point in recharging it.

This left him with a dilemma; being unable to contact Sarah.

The whole incident denoted a bad omen. He shouldn't have left Calgary. Or Sarah. The upcoming flight to Sydney churned in his gut, hurting his head. He was seriously contemplating *not* boarding the midnight flight.

You're not very smart, Taylor. You should never have left her.

He was dining at Urban Crave, an eatery featuring street

food. The burger and chips were delicious, but he fingered the chips, mindlessly picking at the food. He hadn't bought a cold one…*a beer*. His world tilted off course, but he endured the imbalance. He missed Sarah, ached for Sarah. He didn't want to travel. He glanced at his watch. It was 8:00 p.m. The flight left in four hours.

He frowned and pushed the plate aside, having no desire to finish the meal. He had a decision to make in the coming hours and without his phone, he couldn't book a flight to Calgary whether he wanted to or not.

What should I do? He supposed, board the plane and travel to the home that wouldn't feel like a home, *without Sarah*.

TAYLOR WANDERED AIMLESSLY for an hour or so, exploring airport shops, looking at Canadian gifts, maple syrup and candied salmon. He bought a business book, a travel magazine, though his sad mindset had not improved. He went to the gate at ten p.m., two hours before the plane's departure. He stood near a bank of windows, studying his ride, the silver jet: a Boeing 787 Dreamliner. It was massive. It would carry him and two hundred or more passengers across the Pacific Ocean, but not the woman who mattered most. Fourteen hours, two continents and an ocean would separate them. Too many miles to think about.

Taylor sighed while sitting on a seat. Many passengers were in the waiting area. Families. Children running past him like wild animals, screaming banshees. Couples. He could have cried while watching two partners sharing a brief kiss. He sighed, looked away.

"Taylor Quinn, if you're in the waiting area, could you please come to the podium to have your documents verified."

Taylor left his seat and approached the podium. He retrieved his passport and boarding pass from his breast pocket and passed the documents to the agent.

"You're Taylor Quinn?"

"Yes."

The agent reviewed his passport details and perused his boarding pass. "How are you this evening, Mr. Quinn?"

"That's a good question. I'm not sure you want to learn the answer. Some questions lead to responses people don't care to know."

Her eyebrows rose. "That bad, hey? I'm issuing you a new boarding pass."

Taylor didn't understand why a new boarding pass was necessary, but he waited patiently, not saying a word. The agent passed him the pass and he looked at it, seeing his seat assignment had changed. "Business class? Really?" The change didn't improve his surly mood.

The agent nodded. "Smile, Mr. Quinn, your luck has improved. I have happy news. To help you celebrate, we've upgraded you."

"I don't understand. I don't have *anything* to celebrate."

"Someone special will be joining you." The agent smiled like the cat who'd eaten the canary. What information was she holding back?

Confused, Taylor asked, "Who?"

The agent reached for a second boarding pass that was

printing. "You'll know the details shortly, and you'll be grateful. After all, it's a long flight to Sydney and the hours will pass faster while holding your girlfriend's hand." She smirked. "Please give this boarding pass to Sarah. She's arriving on Air Canada Flight 227 at ten."

Taylor's eyes widened. They filled with fluid. "Are you serious?"

"Ten p.m., Gate C43. The flight's on time."

"I…" Taylor gasped, touching his lips. "I can't believe this."

"She tried to message you. She couldn't reach you."

Taylor showed the agent his phone. It was silly, weak of him, but a tear slipped from his eye. "I broke it."

"Well, that's terrible luck, but your fortune is improving. Yes? You can't leave the international terminal, but you may want to meet Sarah at the entry point."

"Thank you," Taylor said. "You've given me the best news. The best news ever."

"You're welcome. It's my pleasure. Have a good evening and a good flight to Sydney, Mr. Quinn.

When Sarah's flight arrived in Vancouver at 9:58 p.m., she only wanted to reach one place and one person: Taylor.

The passengers deplaned slowly. The walkways through the airport were crowded with people. She weaved among them, walking, running, slugging her purse and a backpack on her shoulder. One hour to traverse from the domestic terminal to the international. She rushed, wanting only to reach Taylor as soon as possible, to join him and begin their life together.

After officers reviewed her documents at the checkpoint, she passed through the security line and headed into the international terminal. Someone called her name.

"Sarah—"

She moved toward his voice. When she noticed Taylor, she ran to him and fell into his arms. Taylor grasped her face. He kissed her. "Sarah. Sweet, beautiful Sarah. What have you done? I can't believe you're here."

She clung to him. His eyes filled with emotion, with tears. She wiped them away. "I had to come. I felt lonely after you left. My heart was breaking."

"Mine was hurting, too. But what about your home?"

"What is a home if the man I love isn't in it? Taylor, you're my home. Home is wherever I'm with you. I had to come."

He kissed her forehead. "Sweet, Sarah." He grinned, caressing her cheek. "Are you seriously joining me on the flight to Sydney?"

She nodded. "Yes, I am. But how did you know? I expected I'd be searching for you at the gate."

"The agent surprised me. She gave me your boarding pass." He showed it to her. "We're sitting together in business class. I can't believe it."

"We're going home, Taylor."

"I have no home unless it's with you," Taylor said. "Wherever you go, that's where I want to live."

"We still have much to discuss, lots to decide."

"As long as we do it together."

The flight left on time just after midnight. The plane thrust along the runway at high speed and when it finally lifted into the air, Sarah knew she'd made the right decision. Whatever happened next, her searching had finally given her everything she'd ever wanted.

A partner, her forever love, and a home.

THANK you for reading *A Mountain Leads Home.* If you enjoyed Taylor and Sarah's love story, your honest opinion of their romance will support the author's writing career. Please rate or review this book on your favorite book site, review site, blog, or your own social media properties, and share your opinion with other readers. Thank you!

The premise of this novel is special to me as the plot loosely follows my daughter and son-in-law's love story. Though the fictional events differ from the real-life journey, what is true is one man's desire to travel and snowboard in the Canadian Rockies.

Unfortunately, or fortunately, William experienced an accident at Banff Sunshine Village Ski and Snowboarding Resort. On his first day, he ruptured his spleen and was taken to a trauma unit in Calgary, where he met my daughter who was working as a trauma nurse.

A couple's care for each other blossomed at first sight.

When my daughter asked me for advice, wondering whether she should befriend Will through Facebook, which was a new social media platform at the time, well…given I'm a romance author, I advised my daughter to add Will as a friend. After all, what harm could it do?

Recalling that time, the same advice that brought Will into our home and into our lives took my daughter from me.

Will and Carrie built a life in Australia and married in the fall of 2017 at The Post Hotel in Lake Louise, Alberta, Canada. At the release of this book, their life has taken yet another turn. They're returning to Canada as they purchased a house in Calgary. Hopefully, there's no further snowboarding accidents!

It hasn't been easy with family in two countries, but *love* is worth the sacrifice.

Will and Carrie chose a song for this novel: "*Home*," by Edward Sharpe & the Magnetic Zeros.

Home is wherever love is found.

A *Mountain Leads Home* is the second novel in the Places in the Heart series. Watch for Anne, Laina and Portia's stories, coming soon.

CONTACT SHELLEY KASSIAN

If you would like to learn more about Shelley or her novels, visit her website at shelleykassian.com. Here you can read excerpts from her books, linked reviews, blog posts, as well as discovering her professional affiliations and accreditation.

Follow Shelley in the number one place where readers find free and bestselling books—BookBub.

Shelley enjoys hearing from her readers. If you'd like to contact the author, please send her a message at: shelleykassian@gmail.com.

FOLLOW SHELLEY ON SOCIAL MEDIA

amazon.com/author/shelleykassian

bookbub.com/authors/shelley-kassian

goodreads.com/shelleykassian

facebook.com/ShelleyKassian

instagram.com/shelleykassian

twitter.com/@shelleykassian

linkedin.com/in/shelleykassian

pinterest.com/shelleykassian

ABOUT SHELLEY KASSIAN

Bestselling author Shelley Kassian has been writing timeless love stories filled with romance or dark fantasy (romantasy) for more than twenty years, novels that include her recent true love story, *A Mountain Leads Home*. A history enthusiast, she's traveled far and wide to explore secret gardens and medieval castles, having an avid interest in the Tudor period. Her prose has been described as "near rhapsodic," "pitch perfect," and "stylishly straightforward, rarely relying on complex turns of phrase." Reviewers have said her narrative conveys "imaginative fantasy," "fascinating characters," and "refreshing romance."

Shelley's taken creative writing courses, holds board positions within professional associations, and retains a Professional Editing Certificate. Drawing on her expertise, she has mentored novice writers, but her passion comes alive while scribing her stories into novel-length fiction. Shelley shares her life with her husband, adores her adult children and two grand pups, and when not relaxing at her seaside cottage, lives in Calgary, Alberta, Canada.

www.ingramcontent.com/pod-product-compliance
Lightning Source LLC
Chambersburg PA
CBHW030822210726
48290CB00002B/710